PRAISE FOR
JONATHAN VALIN

"One of the gutsiest private eye writers around."
Chicago Sun-Times Book Week

"Jonathan Valin is in a class by himself... You don't just read one of Valin's Harry Stoner capers, you live through it."
Cincinnati Post

"Jonathan Valin brings energy and wit and language to the 'detective' genre."
—Stanley Elkin

"Travis McGee and his cohorts better move over...Jonathan Valin's Cincinnati shamus, Harry Stoner, is at it again."
Cincinnati Enquirer

"Stoner has cases that still turn out rougher and tougher than anyone else's around."
Hartford Courant

Other Avon Books by
Jonathan Valin

DEAD LETTER
FINAL NOTICE
THE LIME PIT
NATURAL CAUSES

DAY OF WRATH

A HARRY STONER MYSTERY

JONATHAN VALIN

 AVON
PUBLISHERS OF BARD, CAMELOT, DISCUS AND FLARE BOOKS

AVON BOOKS
A division of
The Hearst Corporation
1790 Broadway
New York, New York 10019

The St. Martin's Press edition contains the following
Library of Congress Cataloging in Publication Data:

Valin, Jonathan.
Day of wrath.

I. Title.
PS3572.A4125D3   1982   813'.54   82–1432

First Avon Printing, July, 1983

To Katherine

DAY OF WRATH

1

TROUBLED FACES HAD BEGUN TO LOOK ALIKE TO ME. And people's troubles, too. It was a prejudice I wasn't fully aware of until Mildred Segal walked into my office late one rainy afternoon and I found myself *remembering* her. Not just her air of misgiving or even the depth of trouble behind her light green eyes. I remembered *her.* Details of her life. Grievances, disappointments, sacrifices. Above all, sacrifices. To parents, husband, kids. Mildred Segal had been born for sacrifice, like an island princess. And I suppose I should have felt sorry for her. Only I thought I knew her too well. Thought I knew that behind the abject look was a fierce pride—a victim's canny assurance that, come what might, she would be wronged. It was the next best thing to having a destiny. But I guess I should also have known that people who act like they have a destiny are the only true innocents in the world.

Only I wasn't thinking clearly that April day. I was thinking that I didn't care to deal with the drab, familiar lady sitting in front of me. I was thinking that I wanted to go home to the Delores and drink cold beer and listen to the spring rain pattering against the windows. April just wasn't the right month to delve into someone else's past. Especially the last week of April.

I listened to her anyway. With half an ear. And since I couldn't feel the pity she felt was owed her, I made a show of being polite. I fetched sighs at all the right places. Shook hands with the notion that the world was a theater of injustice. And offered her a cigarette when I couldn't think of anything else to offer up.

"But I don't smoke!" Mildred Segal replied. And then, as if that had been the last straw, she began to cry. "I can't do anything right!" she said helplessly.

I sat there for a moment—staring at her. And slowly, against instinct and judgment and the faint tug of the weather, I found myself feeling exactly what I should have felt the instant she'd walked through the door—deep, authentic pity. She was not an attractive woman —short, flat-chested, with a long, U-shaped, horsey face, pulled down at the mouth, like a horse's mouth, as if she, too, were trained to hold a bit between her teeth. She'd made herself up badly, as well. She was wearing so much eyeliner that her eyes looked as if they had been drawn in ink. And then she'd dressed with awkward solicitude, in a tweed suit that looked to be at least twenty years old. Watching her cry I felt, I think, a little of what women must feel when they see grown men break down. But what finally got to me wasn't Mildred Segal; it was my own hardness of heart. I'd pegged her for martyrdom the moment she'd walked into the office. And the fact that I'd been right depressed me. It just didn't seem fair to Mildred to know what I already knew about her.

So I got up and walked over to her chair—a wad of Kleenex in my right hand and my left hovering about her shoulder in a pantomime of concern. I couldn't quite bring myself to touch her; it would have been too much like kissing a cousin. But I did offer to help—a piece of generosity that I immediately regretted.

"I don't even know if I can afford you," she sobbed. "That's how hopeless I am—coming here and wasting your time and making a fool of myself." She blew her nose noisily, folded up the tissue as if it were a monogrammed towel, and dabbed at her pale green eyes.

"You can afford me," I said half-heartedly. "The question is—do you need me? You haven't really told me why you've come."

"I haven't?" She looked down at the floor as if she'd taken my question as a rebuke. I had the feeling that that was the way she reacted to any question. "It's so personal," she said in a small, dispirited voice.

"Mrs. Segal, most of my cases are personal."

"I suppose that's true," she said. She passed a hand through her short brown hair and sighed. "Yes, I suppose that's true." She finished drying her eyes and looked up at me with a weak smile. "I don't really know very much about detectives—outside of what I've read in books or seen on TV. The fact that I'm here at all is . . . alarming. I had to take a sick day to do it. That'll catch up with me," she said, almost as an afterthought. "One of these days, that'll catch up with me, too. I have this odd feeling that my whole life is about to catch up with me—all the mistakes."

Her smile began to collapse; so I changed the subject, although I wasn't sure if any subject was exempt from her sense of tragedy. She was wired for it, like a switchboard—the remotest line of thought leading straight to her suffering heart. It occurred to me that it had taken

3

considerable courage for a woman like this to come to me at all. It made me think better of her than I had at the start.

"You mentioned sick days?" I said. "Where do you work?"

"I teach school," she said. "Elementary school. They're quite strict about personal holidays. I've already taken both of mine—because of Robbie. So I had to call in sick this morning. I just hope no one saw me downtown, that's all. I don't think I could take any more trouble. I mean, on top of Robbie."

I asked her who Robbie was.

"Why, she's my daughter, of course," Mildred Segal said with surprise, as if it were headline news. "Robbie's my daughter."

"And the trouble she's in?"

She dropped her head to her breast and in a tiny, guilt-ridden voice whispered, "She's run away from home."

2

HOME WAS IN THE NORTHSIDE SUBURB OF ROSELAWN on Eastlawn Drive, an L-shaped, residential street with a large stone church-school set in the bend of the L. Worn, two-story brick houses—each one with its own foursquare patch of lawn, low dividing hedge, narrow asphalt driveway, and maple tree planted in the center of the yard—lined the street on either side of the church. The whole neighborhood had a nervous, conformable, slightly depressed look of probation, as if the presence of that massive church had made the householders stiff and uneasy, forced them to look inside themselves each day and wonder if they'd truly arrived at respectability. From what I could see of the street on that rainy Wednesday afternoon, the time of arrival had come and gone for these families. Everything but the church looked small and haggard and thoroughly sick of pretending to be good.

The Segal home—pitch roof, red brick facade, white colonial trim—was located across from the church on the east side of the drive. I could see a rainswept school yard from the front stoop. A small, lonely looking boy in a knit

5

cap, windbreaker, and jeans was standing in the rain and staring up at one of the basketball hoops as if it were another kind of crucifix. But there were so many emblems of sacrifice up and down Eastlawn Drive that I suppose I could have read an allegory in a Buick. Mildred Segal made sad sense against the backdrop of this middle-class neighborhood. She was the final product of the probationary mentality—a woman so fixed on proving herself before the neighbors that her whole life had taken on the legal, presumptive, and slightly crazy aspects of a trial by jury.

The living room was small and sterile. The furniture —an uncomfortable couch covered with a polished cotton print of yellow flowers on a blue field, two wingback chairs in light blue velvet, a low mahogany coffee table with Queen Anne legs—looked exactly as it must have looked in the showroom. Color-coordinated, fussy, and unlived in. Mildred actually groaned when I sat down on the couch, as if I'd seated myself on an oil painting. Instead of telling me to get up, she ran off to the kitchen to make coffee. And I sat back—rather gingerly—on the sofa, stared out the front window at the boy in the rain, and asked myself what I was doing in a house where the furniture, and apparently just about everything else, was meant for show.

I knew what I'd thought I'd be doing there—taking my own kind of inventory, measuring what it was that Robbie Segal had run away from. But it was fairly clear that I wasn't going to learn much from the visit. At least, not much that I didn't already know. Who wouldn't run away from that living room? I asked myself. Or from a woman whose heart broke when you sat on her chairs? By the time she returned from the kitchen with a coffee pot in her hand, I'd begun to dislike Mildred Segal again and all the strident familiarity of her household. There weren't going to be any surprises here.

"Maybe you'd like some coffee?" she said timidly.

"That would be fine."

"Maybe we should serve it in the kitchen?" she said with a half-strangled amiability and looked greatly relieved when I got up off her couch and walked through an arch that opened on the dining room. The cherry-wood table was set with four immaculate place settings —just as it had been in Pogue's display window. That was one meal that would never be served, I thought, and sighed. I was already beginning to feel sorry for Robbie Segal.

I followed Robbie's mother through another opening into the kitchen. There was a round formica table in the center of the room. Mildred Segal sat down at it abruptly. I guess we camp here, Harry, I said to myself and glanced at the woman. She had a sweet, abstracted smile on her face, as if she'd just looked up from her knitting and found me standing in front of her.

"Do sit down, Mr. Stoner," she said gaily. "And I'll pour you some coffee."

She was happy now. She'd gotten her way. The furniture was intact and I was safely in the kitchen. Everything was swell. I sat down across from her and let her pour me a cup of coffee. Manipulative people make a habit of rewarding you when you go along with their manipulations, like animal trainers slipping a lump of sugar to their beasts.

"Perhaps I should have used the good china," she said, when she caught me staring moodily into the cup. "But they were my grandmother's, and I'd hate to see any of them get chipped."

I felt like throwing the cup against the wall. Instead,

I asked her to tell me about Robbie, and her face bunched up again.

"For chrissake," I said irritably. "We're not going to get anywhere if you keep breaking down."

"Don't snap at me!" she said with sudden vehemence. Then she blushed and said, "I'm sorry. I'm just used to dealing with children all day long. And then Tom, my husband, used to snap at me . . . I don't like men snapping at me."

"Where is Tom?" I asked her.

"Oh, he's dead," she said nonchalantly. "He died eight years ago. Robbie was only six. He died of a stroke in the very chair you're sitting in. From all that snapping, probably." She smiled rather disturbingly. "I was joking, Mr. Stoner. Every once in a while, I make a bad joke. Tom died of arteriosclerosis. For Robbie's sake, I wish he'd survived. To be quite frank, I hadn't bargained on raising a child all by myself. I've done my best, of course, but I've always lacked a certain empathy, if that's the right word. I'm not sure what to call it. It runs in the family, though. My parents weren't particularly warm people. Generous. And supportive. But not empathetic. I didn't expect empathy from them. But this is a different generation. They expect you to communicate in different ways. Ways that I'm simply not equipped to handle. I've done my best, of course. But . . ."

Her lips began to tremble again. "I want to say something," she said heavily, "because I'm probably going to cry, in spite of your warning. And because I know how I must appear to you. I'm not as blind as you think. I know I'm fussy and old-fashioned and not terribly likeable. It is not easy, Mr. Stoner, to go through life knowing that you're not . . . likeable. My marriage suffered from

8

it, and my daughter has suffered from it. And if I may say so, I've suffered from it, too. But that's not what I wanted to tell you." She looked up at me as if the thing she was looking to say was hidden in my face. "I am trying to find a way to express what I feel for Robbie."

"You love her," I said.

Tears spilled out of Mildred Segal's green eyes. "I'm not sure," she whispered guiltily. "I'm not at all sure that I understand what that word means."

I looked down into my coffee cup and said, "That's not a problem I can help you with, Mildred."

But she went on as if she hadn't heard me. "I never wanted a child," she said through her tears. "I never did! I was past thirty when I met Tom. He was fifteen years older than I was. And . . . well, look at me. I haven't had many suitors. I didn't think I wanted any. I had my own apartment. A job. My parents. That seemed sufficient. But then I turned thirty and my parents died and I was alone. A world that I thought was impregnable began to collapse around me, and for the first time in my life I needed help. So when Tom asked me to marry him, I said yes.

"It wasn't love," she said with distaste. "He was well past fifty and in poor health. I just thought a few years with someone I liked, years that would help me get over the loneliness. And I'm sure he was simply looking for someone to take care of him. Which I did. Day in and day out, for eleven years. We never planned on having a family of our own."

She pulled a paper napkin out of a box on the table and rubbed her eyes with it. "I told you I thought my life was catching up with me," she said in a calmer voice. "Perhaps now you can see what I mean. I've done my best for

Robbie. I really have. Perhaps better than most mothers would have been able to do. But there's always been something wrong between us. For some time now, I've felt it would end like this—abruptly, violently."

"Why?" I said. "Why violently?"

"Robbie is short-tempered. Over the last two years she's gone through puberty, and it's made her moody and introverted. Just this week she broke a vase that my mother had given me. It took me three hours to patch it back together. She's become a tyrant around the house. Always breaking my things and shouting at me. That is, when she deigns to speak at all. Adolescence is a kind of madness, I think. Most of the time she's locked upstairs in her room, with that stereo blasting away. I've warned her that the neighbors won't stand for it. Mr. Rostow has already begun to give me odd looks; and we've lived together in harmony for nineteen years. Robbie doesn't care. She says I think too much about the neighbors and too little about her. She says I don't understand her generation. She says I don't understand anything." Mildred Segal looked down at the speckled tile floor and said, "Sometimes I think she's right."

"When did she leave?"

"Four days ago. On Sunday afternoon. We had a fight about a twenty-dollar bill she'd taken from my purse. Then she ran upstairs and locked herself in her room and started playing that stereo as loudly as she could. Instead of sitting there, like I usually do, and fuming, I went out to shop. I was gone about two hours. When I got back at four-thirty, she was gone. She didn't even leave a note. I spent Sunday evening waiting for her to come home. And I stayed home Monday and Tuesday in case she came back during the day."

I took my notebook out of my jacket, flipped it open, and studied the blue lines on a blank page. "You know she'll probably come back on her own," I said, without looking at Mildred. "In a few days she'll probably come back and you can patch it up with her."

"Can't you see that I need to make an effort of some sort?" the woman said. "A gesture. So she'll know that I care."

But the gesture wasn't for Robbie's sake. I knew it and so did Mildred. It was for Mr. Rostow and the nineteen years of neighborliness. It was for Eastlawn Drive and its nervous air of respectability. It was for the world at large, which in this deeply fugitive city prizes nothing more than the show of propriety and the concealment of shame. And it was a little bit for Mildred herself, who had never wanted a child and who was now facing what she thought was the guilty consequence of her own selfishness. Which was just another kind of selfishness, of course. But an understandable kind.

I could have told her that her ambivalence toward Robbie was perfectly normal, that adolescence *is* a kind of madness, that these things happened every day, and that she didn't have to spend a small fortune to prove that she and Robbie were an exceptional case. I could have told her that, but I didn't. First of all, because she didn't want to hear it—didn't want to be told that she was no different than any other stiff-necked parent with a rebellious teenager on her hands. And second, because she wouldn't have understood me if I had said it. It went against the received wisdom of Eastlawn Drive, which said that mothers and daughters must always love one another or, at least, act as if they loved one another, every minute of every day. And that any deviation from

11

that standard was cause for shame. And third, because there was always the chance, remote as it seemed at that moment, that her daughter *had* run straight into trouble.

So I dug a stub of a pencil out of my pocket and began to ask the usual questions. "Do you have any idea where Robbie might have gone?"

"Not the slightest."

"She has no special friends? Boy friends?"

"Well, there's the Caldwell boy," Mildred said distastefully. "Bobby Caldwell. They live on the other side of Eastlawn, across Losantiville near the park. And there's Sylvia Rostow. She lives next door." Mildred's eyes brightened. "She's *such* a nice girl. I just wish that Robbie could be more like her."

I felt a chill run down my spine. When I was a boy, growing up in a neighborhood very much like this one, *my* mother had periodically compared me to the son of a neighbor—a swarthy, pepper-haired, mealy-mouthed kid, who had a genius for pleasing adults. I wrote down Sylvia Rostow's name with an asterisk beside it—to remind me that I wouldn't like her.

"Did Robbie take anything with her when she left?" I asked. "Clothes? Food? More money?"

"No. She didn't take any food or money. I'm not entirely sure about the clothes. I haven't searched her room. If she should come back and found that I'd gone through her things . . ."

"Maybe we better take a look," I said.

At first glance the bedroom didn't tell me anything new about Robbie Segal. Like the rest of the house it was a reflection of the mother rather than of the child—a middle-aged, middle-class dream of adolescence. The four-poster bed was all ruffles and white lace. The furniture—a dresser, vanity table, bedstand, rocking chair—was painted white with gold trim. The carpet was the same pale, fluffy, irreal pelt of blue that you occasionally see on stuffed animals. There were two framed photographs on the vanity table—mom and dad.

It wasn't until I actually stepped into the room—Mildred hovering nervously at my side—that I began to see how wrong everything looked. There wasn't a piece of loose clothing or a book or a record jacket anywhere in sight. The bed had been newly made. The carpet was spotless. Even the stereo on the bedstand had been dusted off and covered with its plastic lid. Either Robbie was an extremely neat young runaway or Mildred hadn't been telling me the truth when she'd said that she'd left Robbie's things untouched.

She must have sensed what I was thinking because she tapped me on the arm and said, in a slightly disingenuous voice, "I *did* do a little cleaning up. After all, with company coming out . . ."

"Mildred," I said. "I'm not company. I'm a private detective. You're paying me money to be here."

"Yes, of course," she said stiffly. "I just picked up a few things."

"Like what?"

"A few of Robbie's things. Nothing important."

I glanced around the room again. It wasn't simply clean; it was denuded, like a hospital room. There weren't any personal items—no posters, no teddy bears, no music boxes, no postcards—none of the paraphernalia that any teenager would surround herself with. It gave me the eerie feeling that no one had ever lived there at all.

"What did you do with them, Mildred?" I said.

13

"With what?" she said innocently.

"All of Robbie's things."

"I can't see where cleaning up a few—"

"Look," I said impatiently, "either you show me what Robbie left behind, or you get another detective. I don't have time to play these games with you."

"Well, really!" she said indignantly and marched over to a closet. She opened the sliding door, bent down, picked up a large cardboard box, then marched back to me. "I'm going downstairs," she said icily. "After all, this is still my house and I can come and go as I please. But I want you to know that I don't like your tone of voice. And I also know that all of this junk"—she thrust the box at me—"was given to Robbie by her so-called friends. I don't understand what kind of distorted impression you want to get of Robbie's home life, but that junk won't tell you a thing about the way I've raised my daughter."

"I'll bear that in mind," I said.

She turned on her heels and walked out of the room. I went over to the bed, put the box on the mattress, and began to sort through the contents. It was like breaking into Pharoah's tomb. Mildred Segal had boxed up her daughter's entire life—everything that Robbie cared for —and stuck it in a closet, safely out of my way. There was a pair of granny glasses with yellow plastic lenses. A gold bracelet with the initials "R.C." on the shank. A necklace with a peace symbol emblem. A black T-shirt with *Pentangle* printed in silvery letters across the breast. A paperback copy of Gurdjieff's *Conversations with Famous People*. A paperback copy of *Everything You Always Wanted to Know About Sex*. A Frederick's of Hollywood catalogue. A ceramic hash pipe that had never been used. An unopened box of Zig-zag papers.

Strawberry incense sticks. A bottle of patchouli oil. A snapshot of a pretty blonde girl in shorts and halter top.

There was a good deal more. But it was all just as innocuous and just as indicative of the kind of life that Robbie Segal had been trying to live in that big, white pillow of a room. It took a perverse imagination to see anything more than a normal teenager's normal adventurousness in any of it. I studied the snapshot and wondered if it was a picture of Robbie. If so, she was a beautiful kid, with long blonde hair and sad blue eyes and a crooked, engaging smile. There was a tenderness and a vulnerability about that face that moved me; but since I'd inched closer to forty, most young faces moved me in the same way.

And, suddenly, I *wanted* to find Robbie Segal. Not for her mother, with all her guilts and proprieties. Not even for Robbie's own sake. But for me. For the opportunity to tell her that the world of Eastlawn Drive was not without end. The feeling only lasted a moment, after which I began to feel foolishly adolescent myself. I knew perfectly well that, like it or not, the girl would have to be brought back home—back to that world without end —and that any sentimental speech about freedom and conformity would sound worse than a lie coming from the man who was taking her back to Mildred. And, at the same time, I knew that I'd probably go ahead and make that speech, if I did find her. To give her what little comfort I could and, perhaps, to console myself for the false positions that life is always forcing us into.

3

I FOUND MILDRED SITTING IN THE KITCHEN, STRAIGHT in her chair—her hands flat on the table, her face unfocused and full of grief. She'd been crying again. Her eyelids were puffy and rimmed with red, and her nose was a little damp at the nostrils. When I sat down across from her, she drew her hands back from the tabletop, like a pianist who'd just finished a piece, and folded them in her lap. Her big green eyes looked so vacant, her long, drawn-out face looked so bereft of hope, that I felt a part of me relent—again. Charity, Harry, I reminded myself. Charity.

"I'm sorry I snapped at you, Mildred," I said.

"That's all right," she said in a forlorn voice. "I deserved it. Imagine putting a clean room before my daughter's safety! I shouldn't have been allowed to have a child."

It sounded like something she'd heard in a movie. A good deal of her conversation did, which is usually the case with people who have no talent for intimacy. I told her, "It's just not that bad."

She shook her head and bit her lip and her green eyes welled with tears. "I don't understand people. Not children or adults. I've tried so hard to please them—to keep everything neat and orderly and livable. But I always end up looking hateful and ridiculous."

I pulled a fresh handkerchief out of my pocket and handed it to her.

"Thanks," she sniffled.

"Maybe if you didn't try quite so hard to please," I said gently.

"I can't help it!" she sobbed and threw her hands up in distress. "I don't know any other way to be."

"I guess not." I stared at her and thought, *all fates are worse than death, Harry.* It was just Mildred's bad fortune to have been born into a world she could never quite tidy up. I patted her on the shoulder and said, "If we're going to avoid these fallings-out, maybe we'd both better be a little more patient with each other."

She nodded heavily and tried to smile.

"I found this photograph in the box," I said, handing her the snapshot of the blonde girl. "Is this Robbie?"

She nodded a second time and her smile blossomed with affection. "She's so beautiful, isn't she? It's a miracle she's mine."

"She is very beautiful," I said.

"Oh, God!" Mildred cried. "I *do* love her, Mr. Stoner. I do. I wouldn't be able to live with myself if anything happened to her."

"Nothing's going to happen to her," I said, even though I knew that I shouldn't have said it. "She's probably in a shelter right now."

"Do you think so?"

I nodded. "There are several dozen shelters and vicarages around the city. I'll run the standard checks in the morning."

"Wouldn't they call me—if she was in a shelter?"

"Not unless Robbie wanted them to," I said.

Her face collapsed. "I see."

"Or she could be staying with a friend or relative."

"Oh, I think I would know by now if she were still in the neighborhood. One of the parents would have called me. Even that dreadful Caldwell man."

"Why do you say the Caldwells are 'dreadful'?"

"Because they're trash," she said severely. "Poor white trash."

I started to chide her, but she held up a finger, as if to say on this matter her prejudices could not be shaken. "They *are* dreadful people, Mr. Stoner. Believe me. Their house is a pigsty; they both dress like hobos; and they haven't a penny to their name. The father lives off Welfare—some kind of mental problem which he claims as a permanent disability."

I thought of the gold bracelet I'd found in Robbie's room, with the initials "R.C." on the shank, and asked her what Caldwell's son, Bobby, did for a living.

"Nothing. He's still in high school, I think. That is, he is when he decides to go to school. From what I can tell, he spends most of his time at home, working on his automobile or playing the guitar. He's actually a good musician—or so Robbie tells me. I think that's the only reason she likes him. They have nothing else in common."

"Does he play professionally?"

"I don't know," Mildred said. "I wouldn't think so, though. He's only sixteen."

I stared at the photograph and said, "Is this a fair likeness of Robbie?"

"Yes."

"Do you know who took the picture?"

"Oh, yes," she said and her eyes brightened again. "That was taken on a picnic with the Rostows. We all went out to Kings Island for the day."

"What does Rostow do for a living?"

"He's in antiques," she said, as if "antiques" were an exclusive men's club.

"And how old is Sylvia?"

"Robbie's age, fourteen. She's *such* a nice girl," Mildred said with that same fulsome warmth. "She and Robbie are very close. I've done my best to encourage their friendship. Little girls need a confidante of their own age, don't you think?"

I told her that she could fit all I knew about little girls in a bug's ear.

"You have no children of your own?" she said with surprise, as if, in Roselawn, children were one of the ten curses.

I shook my head. "Never been married. Although I've come close a couple of times."

"What happened?"

"I don't know, Mildred," I said wearily. "I guess I'm just not marriageable."

"That's ridiculous," she said. "A good looking man like you."

"Why don't we stick to Robbie?"

She flinched as if I'd slapped her. "I was being polite," she said in a wounded voice.

"I know you were, Mildred. That's just not one of my favorite subjects."

"Losing my only daughter is hardly one of mine, you know," she said, with some justice.

We were headed toward another argument. Deep down, in spite of the charity I'd subscribed to a few

19

minutes before, I knew that she and I would always be headed in that direction. People like Mildred were simply too easy to hurt. So I asked her for the addresses of the Caldwell boy and the Rostow girl, copied them down in my notebook, got up, and walked to the door.

"You will call me?" she said as she scurried up behind me.

"I will when I've found something out."

"And you do think she's all right?"

"I told you I did."

"I just couldn't stand it if anything happened to her," she said again and twisted her hands to punctuate the thought.

I was tempted to tell her that what had happened to Robbie had started a long time before she'd run away. But I checked myself. It would have hurt Mildred too deeply. And besides, it was something that she already knew.

4

IT WAS STILL DRIZZLING—A FINE GRAY MIST THAT WET
my face as soon as I stepped out the door. I didn't mind
the damp. After the hour I spent with Mildred in that
dry, cramped house, the weather felt good. I looked back
over my shoulder when I got to the end of the walkway
and saw her peering anxiously out the front window—a
dour, befuddled woman waiting for her only child to
return home. I hadn't told her that there was a slim
chance that Robbie wouldn't be coming home, that her
daughter might have used the money she'd stolen from
her mother's purse—plus whatever else she'd been able
to panhandle or steal—to buy a one-way ticket away
from that drab brick house on that drab brick street.
That it might be months or years before Mildred heard
from her again—a tiny, worn-out voice on the phone
begging for money or a plane ticket home. And what
Mildred would be buying back would be a very different
person than the rebellious teenager who'd run away
from Eastlawn Drive. What she'd be buying back could
have been so damaged and exploited that it might never
raise its head again. Or it might have turned so callous

that it wouldn't think twice of robbing the woman and bolting back into darkness. I hadn't told Mildred that, for the obvious reasons and for some slightly better ones.

What I'd found in that box in the girl's bedroom was one reason. Robbie hadn't taken any of her valuables with her when she'd left. None of the baggage she probably would have taken along, if she'd been planning a long trip. Not that gold bracelet, which she could have pawned for ready money when her own small cash supply ran out. Or the necklace with the peace symbol, which, like a badge or a talisman, might have buoyed her spirits on the long journey out. Or the snapshot I had in my coat pocket—an image of herself she could have looked back on when times were hard. And then there hadn't been any previous flights—none of those sprints into the outside world that usually precede a long-distance run. In fact, the circumstances suggested a sudden, relatively short excursion. Probably to a place so close by that Robbie hadn't felt the need to arm herself with money or with belongings. Probably to a place that was familiar and hospitable—a place she might have dreamed of running to for a long time. A place where all of those dreams she'd been collecting in her upstairs room—that familiar adolescent mix of instinct and idealism—would come to life.

Part of me wished her safe conduct. The part that Mildred Segal had hired trudged on through the weather—past a hedge of rosebushes spangled with raindrops and up an asphalt drive colored with the rainbow hues of motor oil slicks—up to the Frederick Rostow Residence. That was what it said on the lawn, on the chain sign that a plaster statue of a Negro jockey was holding in its rain-soaked hand: Frederick Rostow Residence.

22

I stared at the plaster Negro and felt a little embarrassed for Fred. Even in Cincinnati, that sort of thing had gone out with the Civil Rights Act, although I'd have been willing to bet that there were thirty thousand little Negro jockeys sitting in dark basement corners from Delhi to Indian Hill, like a race of imprisoned elves, waiting to be returned to daylight. And some day it could happen. Cincinnatians knew that. In a way, that was the gist of their native wisdom—some day it could all come back again. Racial prejudice didn't die in this city; it just got stored in the basement with the rest of the supplies.

The Frederick Rostow Residence didn't quite live up to its billing. It was another two-story, red brick house with colonial trim. It did have a bay window in front and some fresh paint on the gutters. Otherwise it was indistinguishable from the other houses on the street. Same foursquare lawn. Same hedge. Same budding maple tree, its trunk blackened in the rain. I walked up to the front door and knocked.

"Just a second!" a cheerful male voice called out.

Someone laughed heartily, then the door opened and a short, smiling man stepped out from behind it. Fred Rostow, if that was who the man was, bore a disconcerting resemblance to Lee Harvey Oswald. A kind of plump, prosperous, untroubled-looking Lee Harvey Oswald, dressed in white leather shoes, gray checkered acrylic slacks, shiny white leather belt, and light blue Izod shirt.

"Howdy!" he said. "I'm Fred Rostow. And you must be the detective Mildred hired."

I did a bit of a double take and said, "I guess I must be."

"Oh, hell, don't take it like that. Mildred was just on the phone with Madge, telling her all about you. And I want you to know we'll be happy to cooperate." He

23

passed his fingers through his short black hair and laughed. "Geez, it's kind of exciting, isn't it?"

I shook my head and thought, Mildred. Just—Mildred. "Robbie Segal's disappeared, Mr. Rostow. Did Mildred tell you that?"

"Oh, yeah," he said cheerfully. "I didn't mean to sound like I was glad she'd run away or anything. I just meant . . . well, you know, meeting a detective and all. You carry a gun?"

"Christ," I said under my breath.

"I mean, on TV, detectives usually carry guns."

"Hold it!" a woman called out from inside the house. And a Magicube went off with a blinding flash. I swiped at the spots before my eyes and heard the woman say, "Just one more!" And there was another flash. Then someone grabbed my hand and pulled me to a chair.

When my eyes cleared, they were both sitting across from me—Fred and Madge—on a long, russet-colored sofa with teak trim. There was a glass and chrome coffee table between us, with an open box of chocolates in its center. A framed lithograph of Picasso's *Don Quixote* was hung on the far wall, above a huge TV. There were several other prints on the walls—Miros and Klees, I thought, although I couldn't be sure with all those spots still dancing before my eyes.

"We like to take pictures," the woman said a bit apologetically. "My mother always said she wished she'd had more pictures of us when we were children."

I nodded politely.

"So she could look back on them, you see?" the man explained.

There was an embarrassed silence, in which the

24

Rostows took account of their lives since childhood and I sat there, on an Eames chair with vinyl cushions, and tried to keep a straight face. They were a pair, all right. The woman with taffy colored, permanently waved hair and the sort of tall, doughy, nonplussed face you see on middle-aged suburban children. And the man with his shaky, weasel's look and his golf club outfit. The woman was wearing black wool slacks and a pearly white blouse. She had an apron tied at her waist with "I hate housework" stitched across it in red letters.

"You might think we're taking this lightly," the man said after a time. "We're not."

The woman shook her head so violently that her eyes crossed. "No, we're not."

"We just know Robbie so well."

"Like our own daughter."

"And we know that she wouldn't . . ."

"Get in any trouble," the woman said.

They were finishing each other's sentences. I didn't know how long I could take it. As soon as they shut their mouths, I asked them if I could talk to their daughter.

"Sure. Of course," they said.

The husband got up and walked out of the room, and the woman fiddled with the tassels on her apron.

"I understand your husband is in the antique business," I said.

"Well, not exactly antiques. Near antiques."

Used furniture, I thought. It helped to explain the banality of that room.

"You don't think Robbie's in any real trouble, do you?" Madge said with a look of concern that made her tall face collapse.

The seriousness of the occasion was catching up with

her, after all the hi-jinks. "I don't know, Mrs. Rostow. You know the girl better than I do."

"I just can't imagine Robbie getting into . . . I mean, she's *such* a nice girl."

I laughed. I couldn't help it.

"Did I say something funny?" Madge Rostow said.

"No," I said in a soothing voice. "You just reminded me of someone else for a moment."

She nodded agreeably, but her brown eyes had grown hostile and a little confused. Never laugh at a burgher, Harry, I said to myself, they just don't know how to take a joke.

Madge Rostow clammed up after that. And we sat there quietly until Fred came back into the room.

"Where's the body?" he said with a grin.

"We've been talking," Madge said with flat, uninflected politeness. And it was as if she'd sent a wordless warning to her husband, who stiffened suddenly and eyed me suspiciously.

"Talking, huh?" he said in his wife's flat, denatured tone of voice. "Well, that's good, I guess." He sat down on the arm of the sofa and patted his wife on the shoulder. She looked up at him and for a moment they communed silently, like two machines sending each other coded messages over the phone.

"How long you been in the business, Mr. Stoner?" the husband said, turning back to me.

"For about twelve years," I said.

"You handle a lot of these kind of cases? Runaways, I mean?"

I told him I'd seen a few. He apparently wanted to see my credentials—that had been the net effect of his wife's communications. I wasn't the welcome visitor any more

26

—the nice detective whose face would be pasted in the album alongside Aunt Jen and Uncle Bill. I was a stranger and, therefore, suspect. There couldn't be a mentality more parochial or xenophobic than that of a suburban householder in a declining neighborhood. I could understand it, too. To have struggled all one's life for such meagre rewards—an Izod shirt, a stitched apron, and a house out of a television sit-com. And to see that little ground slipping away daily. To suspect, in the eyes of a stranger, that it wasn't worth having to begin with. That would set anyone's teeth on edge. Plus, it had begun to dawn on the Rostows that Robbie's disappearance could change their lives, coming, as it did, out of the nightmare world of social and financial reversal that undermined the seeming solidity of every middle-class neighborhood. It could happen to their child, too. It could happen to them. Which was the reason for the sudden cautiousness.

"You'll watch what you say when you talk to Sylvia?" the mother said.

"Of course he will," the man said with false confidence. "Wouldn't want to be putting the wrong ideas in anyone's head."

"Of course not," the woman said.

"I mean, this is a serious business, isn't it? This is a bad thing."

"A bad thing," Madge repeated.

"I blame it on the school system," Fred said. "Now they want another mil of tax money, and they don't even look after our children properly. Our whole society is screwed up, if you ask me. When I was a boy, no one ran away from home. No one wanted to. Home was . . ."

"Everything," the wife said.

"Exactly. Home was everything. You lived there and

27

you died there. And the generations passed through your house. And you got to see people growing old, and they got to see you growing up and another generation coming. Nobody stuck anyone else in nursing homes, to wither and rot. Nobody ever ran away."

"It was all natural," Madge said.

"That's what it was. You learned to accept things—to tolerate things. Differences. To accommodate them for the sake of the family. You *had* to accept them, because you saw yourself everywhere you looked. Like your whole life was happening at once. Bits and pieces of it. Different stages. From birth to death. So how could you not show . . ."

"Charity," Madge Rostow said.

I was moved in spite of the sentimentality of the words and the sing-song way they'd been delivered. And in spite of the fact that things had never really been that way. The Rostows were only voicing their own hopes and the hopes of their beleaguered class. For them, it had all come down to pictures in a photo album—those bits and pieces of a continuous time.

"Well, here she is," Fred said with alarming gaiety. "How you doing, princess?"

Sylvia Rostow ambled into the room, plopped down on a baize chair, and stared at us with undisguised boredom. She was a plump, freckle-faced teenager, with her mother's dirty blonde hair and her father's knife-blade nose and a little, bruised O of a mouth that made her look—and would probably always make her look—as if she'd been sucking on a stick of cinnamon candy. She had on a tartan skirt, knee socks, sneakers, and a schoolgirl's white blouse. And she was chewing a wad of gum so large that it made her pale, white cheek look swollen.

"Get rid of that gum," her mother commanded.

Sylvia pulled a long string of it out of her mouth, then sucked it back in like a strand of spaghetti.

"Young lady," her mother warned her.

Sylvia gave her a look, then reached inside her mouth, pulled out the wad of gum, and plunked it down in a glass ashtray sitting on a table beside her chair.

"Satisfied?" she said, licking the sugar off her fingers.

"You mind your manners," the mother said.

Sylvia made a face, then stared at me. "So you're the detective, huh?"

"I'm the detective," I said.

"You don't look like a detective," she said. "You're too old."

I laughed and Sylvia's mom threw her hands to her head as if she thought she might lose her mind. Fred squirmed on the arm of the sofa.

"Princess," he said.

"Well, geez, Dad," Sylvia said. "I mean, how do you know he's a real detective? He could be just anybody."

Fred looked at his wife as if to say "she's got a point." Sylvia plainly had him wrapped around her pudgy finger. But the mother wasn't taken in for a second.

"Stop being such a smart-aleck, Miss," she said. "Or there's going to be trouble."

"Geez," Sylvia groaned. "O.K. What do you want to ask me?"

I said, "Do you know where your friend Robbie Segal's gone?"

"She's not my friend," she said disdainfully. "Not my *real* friend."

"That's not what I've been told."

"Well, you've been talking to that batty Mildred."

29

"That's it!" Madge Rostow said. "You're grounded for the night."

"Oh, Mom," Sylvia said.

"And if you don't start behaving, it'll be for the week. Your friend Robbie could be in a lot of trouble, whether you know it or not. I want you to tell this man everything he wants to know or there's going to be hell to pay later."

"Robbie can take care of herself," Sylvia said petulantly and gave me an ugly look. "Anyway, I don't know where she went."

"When was the last time you saw her?" I said.

"I don't know. Four days ago, I guess."

"On Sunday?"

"Whatever," Sylvia said.

"In the morning or the afternoon?"

"The morning."

"Did she talk to you about leaving home?"

Sylvia shook her head condescendingly. "No. You could hardly blame her, though."

"Young lady!" the mother barked.

"Well, geez, Mom, everybody knows Mildred's a basket case. I don't know how Robbie put up with her for as long as she did. Always checking up on her and all. Never letting her go out and have any fun."

"What kind of fun?" I said, before Madge could step in again.

"Fun," she said with exasperation. "You know, fun? Like going to parties and dancing and going out with guys."

"I thought she went out with Bobby Caldwell."

Sylvia laughed scornfully. "That fag. They didn't go out, they just hung around together. That's probably where she went—to Faggot Bobby's house. Him and his big deal music."

30

I had the feeling that Sylvia Rostow had been interested in Bobby Caldwell herself, until Robbie had come along and claimed him. She certainly sounded like a jealous girl.

"Did she say she'd be going to Bobby's on Sunday?"

"She didn't have to say it. She's always over there—like some groupie."

"Sylvia," the mother said.

"Well, it's true, Mom. You've said it yourself. If you hang around trash, you become trashy."

The mother ducked her head a bit. "She does seem to spend a lot of time with those trashy people. I really can't understand it. A nice girl like her."

"She's not a nice girl, Mom," Sylvia said with an evil little smile. "Not anymore."

"What does that mean?" I asked.

"Go talk to Bobby," she said. "Ask him what it means."

5

SO I WENT TO ASK BOBBY. WALKED THROUGH THE RAIN
to the intersection of Losantiville Avenue, where Eastlawn Drive dipped down in a long, scythe-shaped curve
before rising again at the edge of Roselawn Park. Across
the intersection, the neighborhood changed character.
The red brick colonials became old yellow brick apartments, with glass block set in their facades and street
addresses written out in big metal numbers fastened to
the brick. The apartments looked like they'd been built
in the late forties, during the postwar boom—low-rent
housing for the soldiers coming home from overseas.
Functional, three- and four-story rectangular brick
buildings, divided into sixteen two-room units with pa-
per-thin walls and pine floors and a bare minimum of
fixtures and appliances, they had never been meant for
show. The developers hadn't even planted trees in the
front yards. Just an occasional hedge, running like a thin
green bunting at the bases of the facades, and a few
scrubby pines growing in the saw-toothed shadows between the buildings. The plain grass lawns stretched,
one after another, down the hill and up to the park,

separated by narrow concrete driveways and by tall, black-stemmed, white-capped gas lamps which had begun to glow a warm yellow against the late afternoon sky.

There was no movement on the street. No cars. No kids. No bird sounds. No street noise. Nothing but the melancholy hiss of the rain and the sputtering yellow lamps and all that damp green lawn and all those mean yellow buildings. It didn't take much exposure to that part of the street to understand Mildred Segal's ferocious sense of propriety. Because this was precisely what she was afraid of. Not poverty, but this lower-middle-class life with the shine rubbed off, with all but the smallest pride in appearances swallowed hard.

At one time the street had probably been home to the auto workers at G.M. and the factory workers at Hilton-Davis. But most blue-collar types were no longer willing to settle for the purely functional decency of these worn buildings. They'd moved on to Sharonville. Or to Montfort Heights. To brand new brick and drywall tenements, with built-in dishwashers and central air and a stylish veneer as thin as the chrome foil on a windshield wiper knob. Only the ones who couldn't afford to choose lived here now. The ones who lived on fixed incomes and couldn't move if they wanted to. The ones stepping up from poverty, for whom lower Eastlawn Drive was a first taste of respectability. And the ones like Pastor C. Caldwell, who were just hiding out.

I found him midway down the block, on the first floor of one of those big yellow nondescript buildings. *Pastor C. Caldwell, 1-D.* Scribbled in pencil on a scrap of paper stuck in a pitted mailbox. The long entry hall smelled of dry-rot. The overhead lights flickered with the current, casting irregular shadows on the patched plaster walls. It didn't look like anyone's idea of paradise—not even a confused and angry teenager's.

There was a peephole buzzer set in the door to 1-D. I pressed the button and a moment later he answered. He was wearing a fresh T-shirt and khaki slacks. No shoes. He held a section of newspaper in his right hand.

"Yes?" he said nervously. "Could I do something for you?"

There was a bit of the Kentucky hills in his voice and a good deal more of flat Midwestern prairie. But the predominant note wasn't regional, unless you wanted to call hopelessness an exclusively urban sound. Pastor C. Caldwell spoke with the tired, shiftless, slightly servile voice of a man who had nothing left to lose. No pride. No property. No dreams. It was a voice that said "I just want to get by."

The face fit the voice. Crew-cut gray hair, diving in front to a widow's peak. Tan, weathered skin. Cheeks hollow where the back teeth had been pulled out. Puckered mouth. Great tufted brows. Puffy eyelids that narrowed to slits and just the gleam of restless blue eyes behind them. There was a day's growth of beard on his chin and neck. He looked to be in his mid-fifties, but given the kind of life he'd probably led, he could have been thirty-nine.

"Could I do something for you?" he said again.

He'd been taking me in, and I could tell from his eyes and his voice that he hadn't quite figured me out yet—whether I could do him any harm. I decided to keep him guessing until I located his son, Bobby, because I had the feeling that he wasn't going to do me any unpaid favors. His world was one of strict and fierce economy—you

34

took what you could get and you took what went with it and you didn't take or give anything else to anyone.

"Is your name Caldwell?" I said in a tough voice.

"Yessir," he said and shuffled his feet.

"You have a son named Bobby?"

"Yessir."

"I'd like to speak to him."

"What about?"

"That's between him and me."

"Bobby ain't in no trouble, is he?" he said.

"No. I just want to ask him a few questions."

"Well, he ain't here. Matter of fact, he stepped out a few hours ago and won't be back till supper time."

"I'll wait," I said and pushed past him into the room.

There was a television going in one corner, with a green vinyl recliner parked in front of it and an ashtray full of butts beside the chair. The rest of that newspaper he was holding was scattered around the room. A piece on the couch—a hideous stained wood and plaid cloth number with a matching coffee table in front of it stained the same tarry black. A piece on the red, oval rug. A piece on the radiator jutting out from the wall. And what wasn't covered with paper was littered with dirty clothes. In fact there was a trail of them leading across the floor to an open closet. The room was exactly what Mildred Segal had said it was. And, like Mildred, I couldn't understand what the pretty blonde girl in the snapshot could have found there to interest her.

I sat down on the sofa and the man went over to the green recliner. He sat down, put his left hand to his mouth, and sucked on it nervously.

"Sometimes it still hurts me," he said. He pulled the hand away from his mouth and held it up. There was a

35

bump of bone where the thumb should have been. "Lost it over to Gibson Cards." He sucked on the bump again. "Their damn machine's what done it to me. Their damn machine's what cost me my livelihood." He said it fiercely, as if he expected an argument. "I told the foreman I wasn't going to work on no machine without the proper training. Not for no lousy two-ten an hour, I wasn't. You know what he said to me. He said, 'You don't got no goddamn choice.' " Pastor Caldwell mused on the injustice of that for a moment. "That machine 'bout tore my hand off. And I ain't been worth a goddamn ever since. Doctor says my nerves are shot. Can't go out. Can't do no work at all.

"Sometimes I can still feel it there," he said, wriggling the stump. "Like I never lost it nor my nerve neither." He sighed heavily. "You know what I think, mister? I hear the preachers on the radio shouting 'Jesus, this' and 'Jesus, that' and send us your money. And the Holy Rollers come to my door with their whole damn family, trying to sell me a Bible. And you know what I say to them. I say, 'It's all a pile of shit.' That's all this life is, too, when you can't keep yourself whole but by cutting your damn hand off for two dollars and a dime."

But he hadn't meant that for the preachers and the Holy Rollers. He'd meant it for me. Partly as an excuse for that catastrophic room and the life he'd been leading in it. And partly as the reason why he hadn't thrown me out. He'd been robbed of his job and his nerve and now anybody who wanted to could come right in and shit all over him. There was enough truth in what he said to make me feel disgusted with myself.

"I'm not a cop, Mr. Caldwell," I told him. "I'm a private detective looking for a girl named Robbie Segal."

36

"Oh, Lord," he said uneasily. "Nothing's happened to that girl, has it?"

"Not that I know of. She's run away from home."

"Oh, Lord," he said again. He wiped his eyes with the back of his hand and took another drag off his cigarette. "She's a good girl, that one. Come from a good home. Hell, she'd come on over here with Bobbie and treat me like I was her own pa. I sure hope nothing's happened to her."

"So do I," I said softly. The room and that broken-down man were getting to me—reminding me of another broken-down man and another lost girl and the terrible thing that had happened to her. The memory made me so uneasy that I stood up. Pastor Caldwell flinched, as if he thought I might strike him.

"Have you seen her this week?" I said. "Any time since Sunday?"

He closed his eyes, trying to remember. "Not since Sunday, I don't think. 'Course Bobby's the one you should talk to. He worships that girl. Worships the ground she walks on. But to answer your question—the last time I saw her was on Sunday afternoon. Out in back with Bobby."

"What were they doing?"

"Bobby was playing her some music, I think. He's got him a little place in the garage back there where he can play, on account of the neighbors don't want to be bothered with the noise."

I glanced at my watch, which was showing five-thirty. "What time do you figure he'll be back, Mr. Caldwell?"

"Six o'clock. He run off to Westwood to pick him up a valve grinder. He works on cars back in the back, too. Makes him a few extra dollars that way. And Lord knows, we can use them."

37

That helped explain the gold bracelet. I looked at the man, who was staring idly at the TV. "You don't have any idea where Robbie's gone, do you, Mr. Caldwell?"

He shook his head and said, "You best talk to Bobby."

Only Bobby didn't show up at six. Or at six-fifteen. And that worried me. Caldwell kept smoking and watching the television. And I started to wonder if he was stringing me along.

"I thought you said he'd be back at six," I finally said to him.

"That's what I thought, too," he said placidly. "Now here comes the CBS News and he ain't here. Somethin' must've delayed him."

I stood up. "I'm going to go out back and wait."

He jerked around on the chair when I got to the door and said, "Don't you go poking through my boy's things, you hear? He won't like it if you do." Then he turned back to the TV.

I walked down the hall to the outside door and stepped into the evening air. The street was already lit for night—gas lamps puddling brightly on the wet concrete, house lights glowing up and down the street. The rain had stopped and a chilly wind had come up from the west, pushing the big dark storm clouds across the sky and whistling through the hedges and the pines. It whipped at my hair and my jacket as soon as I stepped off the porch. I pulled the jacket close to my chest and followed a hedge row to the driveway beside the apartment house. There was enough light coming out of side and rear windows for me to make my way back to the garage—a long slat outbuilding with eight pairs of double doors, each with numbers painted on it in phosphorescent paint.

I found 1-C and 1-D, unlatched the doors, and pulled them open. The 1-D stall was dark and empty. A Buick had recently been parked in 1-C. I could hear the engine ticking and could smell the exhaust fumes. I groped around the empty stall, looking for a light switch, and eventually walked into a string dangling from an overhead fixture. I jerked it down and the right side of the double garage was lit faintly by a forty-watt bulb.

There was an oil spot on the concrete floor, but aside from that the cubicle was clean and orderly. A padlocked metal cabinet stood against the rear wall, with a couple dozen pictures taped to the doors. As I got closer, I could see that most of them were pictures of rock musicians, cut out of magazines. But a few of them were snapshots of a boy whom I took to be Bobby. He was a tall, skinny kid, with shoulder-length brown hair and a little boy's face that made him look childishly sweet, guileless, and a little simple-minded. The kind of kid who could be made to do anything. In two of the photos he was sitting on the porch steps of a frame house, his guitar cradled lovingly in his lap. Two other boys were sitting beside him—both of them in their early twenties, both of them holding musical instruments (guitar, sax) and smiling at the camera. Like Bobby they were long-haired, bright-eyed kids in jeans and workshirts.

The most interesting photograph was taped to a fluorescent light hung above a narrow workbench on the east wall. I didn't notice it until I'd turned to leave. It had been taken on the same porch as the other two photos, but Bobby wasn't in it. Robbie Segal was. She was sitting on a stair, her elbows on her knees, her chin in her hands. A man and a woman were sitting on either side of her —like a family portrait. The man had a long black beard with touches of gray in it, long black hair braided in a ponytail, a black beret slanting across his forehead, wire-rim glasses, and a haughty, fleshless, unsettlingly cold-looking face. He was staring so intently into the camera that it was as if *he* were taking the picture, and not the photographer. On Robbie's left, a middle-aged woman with very short gray hair, cut almost like a crew cut, and a mannish, sappy face was grinning mindlessly at Robbie and the black-haired man. She looked as if she were overjoyed to have been included in the picture—like a punk house mother.

I spent a moment trying to decipher the look on Robbie's face. It wasn't a conventional look of happiness, although she seemed happy. It was more like the look she might have had as she sank into a hot tub at the end of a long day. Her eyes were vague and sleepy; her crooked mouth hung open, as if she were taking a deep, satisfied breath. I thought of the hash pipe I'd found in her room, but she looked more than high. She looked spaced-out, thick-tongued, tripping-stoned, as if she'd just done up junk in both arms. It was a drunken look of contentment, and it worried me.

I peeled the photo off the lamp and stuck it in my pocket. Then I took a closer look at the workbench. I found some Beatles sheet music—"Blue Jay Way," "Rocky Racoon," and "I Am the Walrus"—in the bench drawer, along with two good-sized roaches, a box of flat picks, a nail file, a couple of pencils, a package of guitar strings, and a sheaf of Bobby's own music written out on blank music paper. I flipped on the bench light and took a look at the lyrics. One of them was called "Robbie." The first stanza and chorus went:

Come out, Robbie darling, come out and play,
Tomorrow will be a brand new day,

40

We'll share it together, come what may—
Only promise me, darling, that you'll stay,

Stay by me, stay by me, stay by me.
Don't ever go—back into the night,
Robbie darling, back into the night.

I didn't read the rest. At the bottom of the page a different hand had written the words, "You better" or "Your better." I couldn't tell which. There were also some figures jotted down in the margins. Probably the prices of auto parts.

I put the music back where I'd found it and flipped off the bench light and the overhead fixture. It was fully dark outside. And Robbie was still lost. But, at least, I'd learned something about her friend—a romantic teenager with a sweet, insipid face who wanted to rescue his love from darkness, like Orpheus and Eurydice. I just hoped, if Robbie was with him, that he hadn't taken her back to that black-haired man again. It was hard to tell from a single photograph, but that one had the look of a user to me—the look of a self-styled guru, who could twist an impressionable boy like Bobby around his finger. I didn't want to think about what he could do to the girl, because if she were ripe for Bobby Caldwell's maudlin songs, then she was ripe for picking.

6

I MADE MY WAY BY WINDOW LIGHT BACK UP THE DRIVE-way to the front of the apartment. It was well past seven by my watch and still no sign of Bobby. He might have been keeping an eye on the Segal home, I thought, and spotted me and decided to lay low for awhile. Or Sylvia Rostow might have called him after I'd left her house. Or it might have been that he'd gotten delayed, like his father had said, and that he had no idea where Robbie Segal had gone. The fact that he had a crush on the girl and wrote love songs to her didn't mean that she felt the same way about him—a bitter lesson I could remember learning when I was about Bobby's age. Still, he was my best lead and I wanted the chance to talk to him.

I ducked my head against the icy wind and decided to pay one more visit to Caldwell's apartment before call-ing it a night—to put the fear of the law into Pastor C. in case Bobby did come home later that evening. So I trudged back down that dim, shadowy corridor to the rear apartment and knocked. I could hear the rustle of the newspaper and the cackle of the TV behind the door.

"Yes?" he called out.

"Open up," I said.

He opened the door. "What do you want now?" he said, staring at me coldly. He'd apparently done a bit of thinking while I'd been gone—enough to get a little of his lost nerve back.

"The same thing I wanted before—to talk to your son."

"You know damn well he ain't here." He threw the door open and said, "Or do you want to search my place?"

He was on the verge of making a scene—shouting and whining and bringing in the neighbors.

I jabbed him in the chest with a forefinger and said, "You tell your son when you see him that if he doesn't get in touch with me in the next twenty-four hours, I'm going to get a warrant for his arrest."

"On what charge?" he said slyly.

"Are you kidding? Robbie Segal's been gone for four days. She's a genuine missing person. I can have your son up on statutory rape and felonious abduction by tomorrow night. You think you can make bail on two felony counts, Mr. Caldwell?"

I could almost hear the air going out of him. "What do you want to make trouble for Bobby for?" he whined. "My son never did you no harm. He never done no harm to Robbie, neither. He worships that girl. He'd do anything for her. And she for him. Why can't you just leave them alone?"

"Because she's fourteen years old and her mother wants her back," I said.

He hung his head on his chest and sighed. "Her mother's a good woman, I reckon. But she don't know shit about kids."

You can say that again, I said to myself.

"If he were here, Bobby'd tell you that himself," Caldwell said, warming to the subject. "I may be poor, but I've raised my boy to speak his own mind. When something ain't right, he'll say so—straight out. Why all he's ever tried to do is help that girl. She's so quiet and care-ful-acting most of the time. Bobby just helped her to open up, that's all—to see more of life. If she's with him —and, mind, I ain't saying she is—but if she's with him, you can bet your bottom dollar he'll look after her. And he'll bring her back home, too!"

I started to say something about the marijuana I'd found in the workbench and the look on Robbie's face in the photograph I'd stolen, but I let it pass. Caldwell would have denied it, even if I'd shown him the evidence. And, besides, drugs were a part of growing up. At least they were in the nineteen-eighties.

"And I wasn't lying, neither!" he went on. He'd gotten that head of steam back and I was just too sick of the whole silly business to prick his bubble. "Bobby did too tell me he'd be here directly at six o'clock. He come in here 'bout the time that *Days of Our Lives* started and made him a phone call and then said he had to scoot on over to Westwood Auto Parts to get a valve grinder for the V-8 in his Buick."

"He drives a Buick?" I said with surprise.

"Yep!" Caldwell said proudly. "Bought it off an old woman up on Elbrook. Belonged to her husband. Bobby got him a good deal on that one, I'll tell you. Only she runs a little rough, so he was going to pull the engine and regrind the . . ."

I held up my hand, like a stop sign. "There's a Buick parked in the stall next to yours right now."

Caldwell contracted his brow into furrows and rubbed violently at his chin. "Well, that's mighty strange," he said. "Bobby must have come back then, after all. The folks in 1-C don't have a car, so they let him use their space for repair work." He sucked nervously on his stump of a thumb. "Wonder why he didn't come in and eat. We generally have supper 'bout this time. Fact is, I asked him to pick me up some chicken on his way home."

I sighed aloud and stared down that gloomy hallway. It was starting to look too goddamn familiar to me. "Oh, hell," I said to the man. "I'd better take another look. I might as well get the license plate number while I'm out here."

"My son ain't hiding from you!" he said loudly. "I told you he's an honest boy."

I pushed by him out the door.

It was a helluva lot darker on the second trip back. The folks in Caldwell's building must have gone to bed very early, because this time there was just a smattering of window lights to guide me. Plus it had begun to drizzle again—an ice-cold rain that was being kicked along by the wind. I was soaked through and frozen by the time I got to the garage door.

I pulled it open, found the overhead light, and clicked it on. The Buick was still there in the left stall—a '72 Electra painted maroon and white, with a pair of sponge dice hanging from the rear-view mirror and a plastic St. Christopher sitting on the dash. I walked around to the trunk to get the license plate number, then peered in through the passenger's side window. There was blood smeared on the seat cushion—so much of it that it made

45

me weak-kneed. For a moment I just gawked in disbelief. Then I tried the handle, but the door was locked. I ran around the Buick, yanking on the other doors. It wasn't until I got to the rear window on the driver's side that I saw it on the floor, wedged between the seats. The way it had been twisted about, it hardly looked human. But then it wasn't human any more.

I stared at it for half a second, hoping it would resolve itself into a different shape, like a bizarre Gestalt experiment—now a dead body, now a sack of coal. But there was too much flesh and blood and fractured bone showing for it to be anything other than what it was. I couldn't see the head, which was wrapped in something white. Just the torso and the legs. The legs were lying at an impossible angle, flexed backward as if the knees were on the wrong side of the joint, like an ostrich's legs. I felt my stomach rub against my spine and backed slowly out of the garage.

All the way up the driveway—through the wet and the dark—I kept fighting the feeling that what I had seen wasn't real, that I had suffered a dreadful and preposterous hallucination. Even the professional part of me—the part that had learned to look on violent death with a cold eye—rebelled against the fact of that body. It simply didn't belong in that car, in that garage, in a case that had begun in Mildred Segal's fussy living room, on a sedate and unexceptional street.

That shock and confusion must have been written on my face because Caldwell blanched when he saw me.

"There's been some trouble," I told him. "I'm going to have to use your phone."

"What trouble?" he said nervously. "What's wrong? Has something happened to my boy?"

"I don't know. Where's the phone."

He pointed shakily toward the dinette. "On the wall, in there."

I went into the dinette, found the phone and dialed Central Station. Caldwell followed me in. His face had gone as white as my own.

"My boy?" he said hysterically. "Has something happened to my boy?"

I turned to him and said, "There's a good deal of blood back there. It looks as if someone was badly hurt and left in the car."

He covered his mouth with his hands and began to shake his head, very slowly. Back and forth. "Can't be," he said thickly. "Can't be. Can't be. Lord wouldn't let this happen. Not to Bobby. Pray Jesus, not to Bobby."

"I don't know if it is Bobby," I said and realized that my voice sounded panicky, too.

Caldwell stopped shaking his head and his narrow eyes popped wide open. "Oh, Lord," he whispered. "Not the girl."

"I don't know," I said and then someone came on the line.

As soon as I turned back to the phone, Caldwell let out an animal yelp—like the sound a dog makes when you step on its foot. He threw both hands to his mouth as if he were afraid he might scream again, then ran from the room—arms akimbo, hands on his mouth, eyes wide in terror. I saw him race through the apartment door and heard him running down the hall. When I'd finished telling the cops where we were, I ran after him. I found him in the garage, kneeling by the car and yanking helplessly at the door handle.

7

I DIDN'T THINK ABOUT ANYTHING FOR THE NEXT HALF
hour or so—while the forensic team did their work. Not
even about the impossible and terrible way the case had
changed. A case that should have been settled without
any violence at all. A case that was as ordinary as Eastlawn Drive. For a time, I didn't even think about Mildred or about the possibility that what was lying in that
car—a bleeding remnant—could have belonged to her.
I didn't think about Caldwell, either, who had collapsed
and been taken to a hospital when the police finally
cracked open the car door and pulled what was packed
inside into the light.

I hadn't looked at it long, although I knew I wouldn't
forget it. You don't forget torture slayings. They stick
with you always, like your very first glimpse of death.
The head had been wrapped in white adhesive tape—
from crown to chin, like a mummy. Probably to prevent
the boy from seeing what was going to happen to him
next. There were terrible rope burns on his wrists and
ankles, where he'd writhed against whatever he'd been
tied to. When the cops unwrapped his head, they found

48

a bloody dish towel stuffed in his mouth. A dish towel.

I'd watched them lift what was left of Bobby Caldwell into a collapsible gurney, cover it with a blanket, and wheel it off to an ambulance. And when it was gone, I got up and walked back through the dark—pushing my way past cops and white-faced bystanders, until I was far enough away from that garage, far enough down the street, that what had happened there seemed like someone else's trouble—just a cluster of ambulance lights and police cars in a driveway.

I stood in the rain for about ten minutes, then walked slowly back to the apartment house—hands in my coat pockets. I knew there was a particular reason for what had happened to Bobby Caldwell. Bad company, cross words, a rash act. I'd find that part out, I thought. The part that was dreadfully ordinary, the part that hadn't been scheduled years in advance on someone's secret agenda. I'd find it out because it might lead me to Robbie Segal. Because it had become part of the job. And because I wanted to find it out.

Most of the cops had left by the time I reached the apartment building. The bystanders had gone to sleep, if they could sleep after what they'd seen. And the street had settled into rain-soaked decrepitude. I found a police detective standing on the front lawn—or he found me. I told him the story once again, and he listened with that impassivity that cops and adolescent boys confuse with cool and courage. He was a veteran cop, this one, with a shock of white hair and a thick-jowled, heavy-lidded face and a boozer's red, blue-veined, bulbous nose. He looked, I thought, like a short, fat Tip O'Neil. And he sounded like James Cagney—cocky, shrill, and tough. He had a pint of Johnny Walker in his overcoat, and we both took swigs from it as we walked down that miserable hallway to Caldwell's apartment. It wasn't until the liquor hit me that I realized how wet and cold and thoroughly played out I was.

I sat down on the couch, while the cop, whose name was Bannock, pawed around in the dinette. The TV was still on. It was Tom Snyder time, by Pastor Caldwell's clock. I watched that rude, impatient man bait some fool rock musician and felt the whole weight of the day fall on me like a tower. I felt like throttling Tom Synder. Instead I got up and turned off the set. Bannock came back into the living room with a stack of papers in his arms and sat down across from me on the green recliner.

"Don't like Tommie, huh?" he said, spreading some of the papers on the floor in front of him.

"What did you find?" I asked.

"Bills." He let the rest of the papers spill from his hands to the floor. "Mountains of 'em." He toed at the papers. "Question is—what did *you* find?"

I thought about the photo I'd taken from the bench light and said, "Nothing."

"You sure of that, huh?"

"I'm sure."

"Well, we'll probably find out that you're lying," he said lazily. "You do tell lies, don't you? Every once in awhile?"

"Once in awhile."

"Yeah, I heard that about you, boy-o." The little man shrugged. "But what the hell do I care, huh? There are so many fingerprints in that Buick we're bound to score somebody's number. Probably some wacked-out biker with a grudge. They go in for these kind of theatrics."

"Could be," I said.

"Fucking amateurs," Bannock said with spite. "I'm too old to be pulling this kind of duty. Too old and too fat."

Bannock slipped the pint bottle out of his pocket, took a swig, corked it, and tossed it over to me. "Man," he said. "You look like shit."

"I feel like shit," I said wearily and emptied the bottle.

The little man eyed me for a moment, then said, "Go home, boy-o. Go home and forget this whole thing. It'll make you crazy if you don't. I know. It'll make you fucking crazy."

I went home. Walked up Eastlawn Drive to the church yard, got in the Pinto, and drove away from that depressing street with its worn brick houses. When I got back to my apartment in the Delores, I drained another half-pint of Scotch and went to sleep on the living room couch. I must have gotten up during the night and found my way to the bedroom. I didn't remember doing it when I woke up the next morning. But then I didn't remember my dreams, either.

8

ONLY DREAMS HAVE A WAY OF LINGERING WITH YOU
throughout the day—they resolve themselves into a
mood, then someone says something or you see something and a bit of dream precipitates out into the sunlight to astonish you, like finding money on the sidewalk.
It didn't take me long to figure out what was bothering
me that Thursday morning. The newspaper was full of
it—pictures of the body being wheeled to the ambulance
and rows of shocked faces staring at it. Those faces had
been in my dreams. And when I dressed, I found the two
snapshots of Robbie Segal in my sports coat and realized
that she'd been in my dreams, too. She and her two
middle-aged friends—the man with the cruel, fleshless
face and the simpering woman with gray hair. Then
Mildred called—for the first time that morning—and
most of it came back to me in a rush. That brick spec-
trum of a street, shifting gradually from affluence to poverty. The churchyard and the boy standing in the rain.
The garage with the bloody automobile. And Robbie and
me and her mother standing by the workbench, while
the graying woman and her evil friend wrapped the

52

Caldwell boy in white adhesive tape—rolls of it. Then we'd cut the tape away, with those shocked bystanders looking on. But I couldn't remember what we'd found underneath the bandages. Only that I'd been surprised at what we'd seen.

I was sitting on the living room couch, drinking coffee and thinking about what it might have been that had surprised me, when Mildred called for the second time. The first time I'd spoken to her, I'd spent the better part of ten minutes calming her down, assuring her that Caldwell's murder didn't necessarily mean that anything had happened to her daughter. I wasn't sure I believed what I was telling her, especially after what Pastor Caldwell had said about Robbie and his son. But it would have been lunacy to let the woman in on that. She'd hung up, moaning over "poor" Bobby and begging me to make Robbie's safety my first priority. The second call, I thought, was just to make sure that the first call had had its effect. Mildred was undoubtedly one of those people who dialed a busy signal twice—to make sure she hadn't dialed incorrectly the first time.

"You'll keep looking for her," she said, after I'd spent another ten minutes soothing her.

"I told you I would."

"But how? Where will you look? With Bobby dead, where will you go?"

It was a good question. "I'll check the shelters and vicarages," I said. "Just in case Bobby wasn't involved in Robbie's disappearance. And I'll contact the police."

"Yes. What else?"

"I have some other leads, Mildred," I said uneasily, although the photograph was my only real lead—and not a very solid one at that. "Do you know where Bobby

53

and your daughter went when they were together?"

"I don't know that they 'went' anywhere," she said stiffly. "It was my impression that she listened to him play the guitar. Nothing more."

Nothing more, I thought. I wondered, for a second, if she really believed that or if she was trying to find out what I believed. It was a hell of a way to learn what your kid was up to. But then Mildred didn't really care about what Robbie had been up to, as long as she could get her safely back in that overstuffed room without letting the neighbors know where she'd been. Which wasn't being entirely fair to Mildred, who did love Robbie in her own way. But then I wasn't in a fair-minded mood.

"I'll call you when I have something to report," I said.

"Yes," she said mournfully. "Call me. I'll be at home. I couldn't teach today—not after what happened to poor Bobby. Is Caldwell . . . how is he taking it?"

"He collapsed," I said. "He's in the hospital."

"I think I would die," Mildred said. "To see your only child—"

"Stop it," I said with disgust. "Just yesterday you were telling me what trash they both were."

"It may surprise you to know this, Mr. Stoner," she said with assumed dignity, "but in spite of what I said, I didn't wish either one of them harm. And I am truly sorry for their misfortune. But I'm certainly not going to take the blame for it. Or feel guilty for thinking what was true—that they lived like animals."

"They're the ones who are taking the blame for it, right, Mildred? They got what they deserved."

"What a wicked thing to say!" she cried. "I'm sorry I came to you. I'm sorry that I need you at all."

She hung up. But I knew she'd call back. She'd had her

melodramatic moment and she'd repent, like any good stock character, and beg my forgiveness. And I'd forgive her, because, though she hadn't known it, I *didn't* have much patience with people like Mildred Segal. That morning I felt as if I'd seen enough Mildred Segals to last me a lifetime. Men and women who assumed blithely that what they had was the best thing to have and that there was only one way of getting it—the American way of legalized repression and sublimation through status. If that was the way Mildred's society was run, then she should have been forced to see all of it. To see what I'd seen the night before in that bloody garage—the dirty little secret at the heart of her repressions and sublimations, the violence that would keep festering and erupting until it engulfed her whole goddamn world. And the funny part was that she never would see it, never would understand why the world was turning against her—just as she really didn't understand why her daughter had run away. She was so fixed on her own values—on maintaining what she had and on living out the lie of unruffled prosperity—that she would never see that there wasn't room enough for that kind of prosperity and true charity. Maybe when I'd brought her daughter back to her, kicking and screaming, there'd be a bit of judgment, because that's what Mildred and the Rostows and the rest of their kind needed—a day of wrath.

I went into the kitchen and fixed myself breakfast and, after a time, I calmed down. I knew it was the Caldwell boy's murder that had awakened the intemperate Puritan in me. It wasn't just the violence of his death. I'd seen my share of that, in the army and in my job. I could even accept it as a solution to certain problems. And I didn't have much more patience with people who couldn't admit that possibility as real than I had for Mildred Segal and her never-never land of hollow prosperity. It wasn't just Mildred's world that had homicide as its root secret. We all lived in that world—ineluctably. Some of us just lived a little closer to the core of it than others did. I guess, finally, that was what was bothering me. On that particular morning, with those bad dreams in my head, I didn't like the life I was leading. On that particular morning, I think I would have traded it gladly for a wife and a child and steady, interesting work—although that was probably asking too much.

I stared out the living room window at Burnet Avenue. The storm clouds had blown away during the night, and the trees and the grass and the cars parked on the street had a freshly washed bloom. It was a beautiful April day, and I felt as if I had to gird myself to go out into it—like a man in armor—weighed down by what I'd seen and by what I was trying to forget.

I'd just finished my third cup of coffee and started for the door when Mildred called to make peace.

I got to my office in the Riorley Building about nine-thirty and, after checking the answerphone to see if there had been any further urgent messages from Mildred, I pulled the phone book out of my desk and looked up the number of Community Services on Auburn Avenue. I wanted to talk to Frances Shelley—an aggressive young social worker whom I'd worked with before on runaway cases. But she wasn't in.

I got her supervisor instead—a smooth-talking customer named Allan Washington. I'd worked for Welfare myself for a couple of summers when I was in college, so I had a pretty good idea of who I was dealing with—a hard-nosed, middle-aged civil servant, who'd spent twenty years in the field getting all the pity and enthusiasm knocked out of him and whose smooth, rich, amiable voice was probably the only charitable part he had left. Frances was only twenty-six. She hadn't bottomed out yet on all the cruelty and toadying and shameless jockeying for dollars that she'd met with in the field and in the office. She would bottom out, though. It's an odd thing about social work—how, inevitably, the bureaucracy comes to mimic its nemesis, how it takes on the mean-spirited, stingy, transparently manipulative qualities of the worst segment of its clientele, and how the case workers end up feeling just as impotent and angry, just as fundamentally poor, as the men and women they service.

I knew I wasn't going to get the kind of help I wanted from Al Washington, not after he'd found out that I couldn't do him any good. And I also knew that if I left a personal message for Frances it would be marked down against her. Civil servants frown on personal calls made on government time and get their jollies by catching subordinates in just those kind of lapses. It's all a little like the peacetime army, where pettiness substitutes for discipline and grudges are paid out in monthly fitness reports. So I pretended I was still with the D.A.'s office and that I needed to talk to Frances about one of her cases. The smack of official interest got Washington's attention.

"Are you sure this isn't something *I* could help you with?" he said with faintly oily cheer.

I told him, no. That it really wasn't urgent enough to justify his involvement. A minor matter, actually. A question of a record. That shut him down like a thrown switch.

"I see," he said curtly. "Well, Miss Shelley isn't here. She checked out this morning at nine and probably won't be back in the office today."

"Is there someplace I could reach her?" I said. "In the field?"

"Try the Dalton Street Community Center," he said and hung up.

I got the number of the Community Center from the phone book. The black girl who answered my call told me that Frances wasn't in but that she was supposed to be back around noon to supervise a senior citizen's workshop.

"She going to be mighty busy, though," the girl said. "Is it something I can do for you?"

"'Fraid not," I said. "Just tell her Harry Stoner called and that I need to talk to her."

I could hear her pencilling down the message. "Harry Sloaner got to talk to you," she read back.

"Close enough," I said. "Tell her I'll stop in around twelve-thirty."

"Twelfth-thirty," she said.

After hanging up, I spent a few minutes going through the mail and a few more minutes straightening up the desk. And when I'd finished my housekeeping, I got back to the matter at hand—the disappearance of Robbie Segal. Since the two photographs were the only evidence I had, I took them out again and studied them, hoping to spot something I'd missed the first time around —like a name tag or a street address. I wasn't that lucky, although I did end up with a slightly different impression of the girl.

In the first photo, she looked heart-breakingly young and pretty—a blonde teenager with a sweet, vulnerable

58

face. She wasn't any less pretty in the second photo, but something about her good looks had changed. The day before I'd thought that she might have been on drugs—that that was what accounted for the faraway look in her eyes and the breathlessness of her mouth. This time around, it occurred to me that it wasn't as if something had been taken away from her expression—some conscious intensity—rather that something had been added to it, something sensuous and charged, something which made her look less childlike and vulnerable. I thought about what Sylvia Rostow had said—about Robbie no longer being a "good girl"—and wondered if that was what I was seeing: the sudden addition of sexual passion to an adolescent beauty. It made me feel vaguely chauvinist to even consider it, especially since I knew that I wouldn't have spotted the same thing in Bobby Caldwell's face. Maybe it was a charge that *I* was adding, I thought. A bit of semiconscious wish fulfillment. Because the truth was the girl was stunning-looking.

It wasn't hard to understand Bobby Caldwell and his songs. This was a beauty that songs were destined to be written about.

Only thinking about Bobby Caldwell made me nervous. I had no proof that he'd helped Robbie run away. Just a strong suspicion. And no proof that his murder had anything to do with the girl, either. But if the two events were related, my blonde runaway was in very bad trouble. The possibility was ugly enough to get me going again—off that cracked leather chair and out of the office.

I took the elevator down to the main floor, walked through the Riorley lobby—an ornate, rather dilapidated example of twenties American rococo, full of brass chevrons and marble pilasters—to Walnut Street. I picked up the Pinto in the Parkade and drove through the blue April morning, up the Parkway to the Police Building.

It was about eleven-fifteen when I found a parking place among the crowd of cruisers on Ezzard Charles Drive. I locked the Pinto and walked up the sidewalk to that yellowish, foreshortened building, with its flagpole on the lawn and its brick and metal sign by the door. The flag was hanging at half-mast on that windless morning, curled like wet wash about the pole. Someone on the force or someone in the city government had died; and that was the memorial, a red and white banner hanging listlessly against the deep blue sky. In spite of myself, I thought of Bobby Caldwell again and carried that thought with me into the building.

I found a desk sergeant whom I knew, got tagged, and went up to the second floor. I stopped briefly at Al Foster's office—just to say hello—then walked down the corridor to the homicide squad room. Arthur Bannock was sitting at one of the varnished oak tables, chewing out a uniformed patrolman who was standing nervously in front of him, shifting his weight from one foot to the other and rotating his cap in his hands. I waited until Bannock had finished and the patrolman had brushed by me. Someone was going to pay for that chewing out. I could see it in his eyes—a look like murder. Bannock leaned back in the chair and watched him go—his hands behind his head, the tip of a yellow toothpick bobbing in the corner of his mouth.

"Buy you a drink?" he said, pointing to the chair beside his desk.

"It's a little early in the day for me."

He gave me a disgusted look and shook his white

60

head. "What's happening to our country?" he said mournfully. He pulled a handkerchief out of his coat, scrubbed his red boozer's nose, examined the handkerchief, folded it up, pocketed it, spit out the toothpick, and pulled a pint flask from a desk drawer. He raised it like a toast glass. "The hell with you!" he said cheerfully and took a long pull of whiskey. "Now what do you want, boy-o? I know you want something for nothing, seeing that it's too early in the day for you to drink with me."

I took the first photograph of Robbie Segal out of my jacket and handed it to him.

Bannock pinched his lower lip between his fingers and studied the picture. "Very pretty," he said. "You want to see some of mine?"

"Her name is Robbie Segal," I said. "She's a runaway."

"Yeah, well, my heart bleeds, you know? But I got other things on my mind." He passed the picture to me. When I told him Robbie was Bobby Caldwell's girlfriend, he pulled his hand back and took another look.

"His girlfriend, huh?" he said. "When did you say she'd left home?"

"On Sunday afternoon. As far as I can make out, Caldwell was the last person she saw that day."

"Why show this to me?" he said after a time. "Why not go down to Missing Persons?"

"I got the impression that the Caldwell kid and Robbie were very close."

"How close?"

"They might have been lovers," I said. "She might have run away to be with him."

"There was no sign a girl had been living in the apartment," Bannock said.

"She wasn't at the apartment. He must have taken her

61

somewhere else." I took the second photo out of my coat. "To these people, maybe."

Bannock studied the second photo. "Why them?" he said, flicking it with his thumb.

"I don't know why," I said. "It's my guess they were friends of Bobby's."

"This guy must be thirty-five, forty years old," Bannock said.

"You know as well as I do that most runaways end up with adults. Especially if the adults give them shelter and unqualified approval."

"And a few other things," Bannock said sourly. "I suppose you know we found some pictures of this pair in that garage."

I tried to look surprised and pleased.

"Jesus!" Bannock said with disgust. "Take it easy. I'm not giving out awards today."

I laughed. "Who are they?"

"We don't know. Got no record of either one of them."

"Nothing connecting them with the prints you found in the garage?"

"Nothing, period," Bannock said. "We haven't raised a ghost with those prints. And nobody on the street saw a getaway car or anything else. I'm beginning to think that whoever took the Buick back to the garage must have escaped on foot—maybe through the back yards."

"Do you have any idea why the car was driven to the garage in the first place?"

"No," he said. "Although it was as good a place as any to leave the body, assuming that they could get away with it. Which they apparently have. If you hadn't gone poking around there, Caldwell could still be sitting in the car, with nothing to connect him up with anyone.

Except those damn prints. My Lord, they're all over the place, like they didn't give a shit what they touched."

"Amateurs," I said.

He nodded wearily. "Rank amateurs. No criminal records. No Army records. No FBI. No nothing. They killed the poor son-of-a-bitch and couldn't think of anything better to do than take him home. Like it was goddamn prom night." Bannock took another look at the picture of Robbie Segal. "You think she was with him?"

"I think he helped her run away from home," I said carefully. "After that, I don't know what happened, although it would be hard to believe that the Caldwell kid hadn't been in touch with her since Sunday or that if he thought he was in trouble he wouldn't have told her about it."

"Are you saying she could be a target, too?"

"I don't know," I said. "It's possible."

"All right," Bannock said. "You talked me into it. I'll put out an APB on the Segal girl. We'll list her as a material witness to a felony. But, boy-o, if this girl comes in from the cold and I don't hear about it—and I mean the minute after you do—I'm going to take it mighty hard. Understand?"

"I understand." I started to get up from the chair and Bannock grabbed me by the wrist. For a man of his size and years, he had an extremely strong grip.

"Stoner," he said softly. "I meant what I said. If you fuck me over on this, there's going to be trouble. I'm not like your pal, Al Foster, boy-o. I don't turn my back if you step out of line and trust that everything'll come out all right in the end. I expect payment for services rendered."

I looked down into that Irish boozer's red, fleshy face

63

and knew that I'd underestimated him, that behind the free drinks and the stagey patter was a dangerous man. Most cops have to learn their brand of toughness the hard way, secreting it over the years like a kind of callus. This one had been born with that callus.

I jerked my arm loose from his grip and said, "I told you I understood."

He smiled with his mouth, but the rest of his face still looked dangerous.

9

THE DALTON STREET COMMUNITY CENTER WAS LOCAT-
ed in the basement of an Episcopal Church on a tired
block of brownstone tenements and storefront groceries.
The neighborhood it served was one of the poorest in the
city—a hodgepodge of nineteenth-century row houses
and frame bungalows jammed together wall-to-wall on
crabbed, salt-whitened streets. I could see into windows
up and down the block, through the muslin curtains into
rooms where women in print housecoats bent over iron-
ing boards and men in T-shirts drank canned beer and
gazed out impassively at the sidewalks. Children blew
noisily in and out of doors—ten and eleven year olds, with
cigarettes in their mouths and faces that were at once too
shrewd and too exhausted to belong to anyone their age.
The street looked pitifully naked in the noon sun. Not
even the buildings cast shadows, as if the walls weren't
really there or only there the way surveyor's lines are set
in turf—to mark the boundaries between inside and out.

The ugly transparency of the street embarrassed me,
made me feel slightly ashamed of my own home and my
own way of life. I ducked my head to the pavement, as

if by not looking at Dalton Street I'd make it disappear, and walked briskly to the church. I didn't look up again until I'd gotten inside. There was a floor sign by the door, with an arrow pointing down a flight of stairs. I followed the arrow to a pair of gym doors. A young black girl wearing a curly Afro wig was sitting at a desk by the doors. From the blank look on her face, she might have been sitting at the console of a space shuttle.

"Yes?" she said as I walked up to her. "Is it something you want?"

She was probably a pretty girl when she wasn't sitting behind that desk. But something about the job was getting to her. It filled her face with caution and made her voice sound snippy and annoyed.

"My name's Harry Stoner," I said. "I called this morning."

"I remember," she said quickly. "I told Miss Shelley what you said and she say to tell you to go on back."

"Through there?" I said, pointing to the doors.

"What you think?" she said irritably.

I walked through the double doors into a big, tiled rec room. There was a platform on the back wall, with a podium and microphone on it. About a hundred folding chairs were set up in rows in front of the platform. The floors were clean and the chairs were neatly arranged. Apparently the festivities weren't scheduled to begin until later in the day. Frances was sitting behind a long, low table to the right of the platform. A plump, gray-haired, black woman, with a spray of violets pinned to the collar of her dress, sat beside her.

"Harry!" Frances called out. "It's good to see you."

"It's good to see you, Frances," I called back.

She turned to the black woman and said, "Excuse me

for a minute, won't you, Mrs. Forest?" The woman nodded pleasantly. Frances stood up and walked across the
room to where I was standing. She carried herself like an
athlete—a bouncy, masculine kind of swagger that was
part tomboy, part challenge. Frances Shelley was a
woman who meant business. She looked like business,
too. Brown hair cut in a wedge; blue eyes aswim behind
thick glasses; lean unmade-up face; and the petite, wiry
build of a long distance runner.

"What can I do for you?" she said in her exuberant
voice.

"What do you think?"

"I think you're working on another runaway case," she
said drily.

I took the photograph of Robbie and her two friends
out of my jacket and handed it to her.

"She's a very pretty girl," Frances Shelley said. "How
old is she? Thirteen? Fourteen?"

"Old enough to get herself into serious trouble," I
said.

I explained the case to her, beginning with Mildred
and ending with Bobby Caldwell's murder. She shivered
a little when I told her what I'd found in the Buick.

"Shouldn't you take this to the police?" she said.

"I've already been to the cops. They're putting out an
APB on the Segal girl. But the fact is that I don't really
know how deeply involved she was with Bobby Caldwell. Her disappearance could be totally unrelated to his
murder."

"I see," she said abstractedly. She was still staring at
the photograph of Robbie. "Well, I'll run a check for you,
Harry. But we have our own procedures. And if the girl
isn't ready to go home . . ."

"I understand, Frances," I said. "All I want to do at the moment is make sure she's safe."

A crowd of people began filing through the doors behind us—elderly men and women dressed in their Sunday best. Some of them smiled at Frances and me; and one bright-eyed old woman in a straw hat and belted orange suit wagged her finger at us. Frances grinned.

"I don't know where they get their enthusiasm from," she said. "Have you taken a close look at that street out there?"

"Close enough," I said.

"Most of them are living on social security in one-room apartments. They have to contend with inflation, disease, neglect, Reaganomics, and that street. And they still show up once a week to play bingo and listen to a lecturer tell them about all the opportunities they're missing." Frances stared at me solemnly. "I don't think I want to get that old, Harry. I don't think I'm that brave."

I patted her cheek and said, "Yes, you are."

She smiled. "It's just the job, you know," she said and gave my hand an affectionate squeeze. "I'll call you tonight after I've run the check on your Miss Segal." She handed the photograph back to me, started to walk away, then turned around. "I guess I better tell you something else," she said. "The woman in that photograph—the one with the gray hair?"

"Yes."

Frances bit her lip. "I think I know her from some place."

"Well, come on, Frances," I said. "Where the hell is that?"

"A club I used to go to," she said. "I think I've seen her there. A club in Mt. Adams."

"What club?"

"Just a club," she said. "A club I used to go to a couple of years ago."

"Why the mystery?" I said to her. "Finding that woman could be important. Tell me the name of the club and I'll check it out."

"Harry," she said flatly. "It's not that easy. This is a private club. A club for women."

"I see," I said.

"Well, don't look so shocked," she said, although I wasn't looking particularly shocked. "I have a right to my own life."

"Who said differently?"

"I can't really talk about it now," she said, glancing over her shoulder at her flock. "Tonight . . . when I call you about this other thing, I'll explain it to you."

"You don't need to explain," I said.

But she'd already turned away and walked back to the table.

About thirty minutes later I was driving down East-lawn Drive—past the school yard, filled at that hour with children, past the huge stone church, looking gray and grave in the afternoon sun. The shadow of the stone crucifix above the rectory stretched across the pavement, touching the edge of Mildred Segal's front lawn. No one stared aimlessly out of the windows on this street. Children at play looked their ages or a bit younger—cowed, perhaps, by the priests in their black soutanes, who stood like dark pillars among them. Nothing was open or transparent here—not the houses with their long brick faces or the people who lived inside them. It was all shade and privacy—each yard with its own maple tree, like a maze to prying eyes. And yet a boy from this street had been brutally murdered. A girl from these modest houses had bolted to a different life. And in spite of the facade there wasn't any real shade to be found, except for the heavy, mordant shadow creeping across Mildred's lawn.

I simply couldn't get him out of my mind—Bobby Caldwell. The way his legs had been bent back against themselves. The look on his face when the cops had unwrapped the tape. It had shaken me through. Made me weary of all the mean streets and all the hapless people who lived on them. Like Frances Shelley, whose cheek I had patted, I was beginning to think that I wasn't tough enough for the job. Or for what I might find at the end of it. I'd been contracting myself out too long— fighting other people's battles and braving other people's losses. I stared up at Mildred's front door and thought, what if the girl was dead, too. What then?

But there was no one around to pat me on the cheek. No one but me.

Mildred answered the door on my third knock. And when she saw who it was, she ducked her head.

"Are we still on speaking terms?" she said quietly.

"I'm sorry about this morning," I told her. "It was the boy's murder. It shook me up."

She looked at me with surprise. "I wouldn't think that a man like you could be upset by such things."

"Men like me can be upset by any number of things."

"You're an odd person, Harry," she said. "It's taken me a while to see it, because when something's odd, I generally assume that it's me." She held out her hand and said, "Truce?"

"Truce."

"Well, come in then. Don't let's give the neighbors anything more to talk about."

I stepped into the room.

"Nothing's happened to Robbie?" she said, the moment after she'd shut the door.

I told her no.

"It's only that you look . . . I don't know, you look so discouraged."

"It's just the job, Mildred," I said.

"Yes," she said after a moment. "I suppose it must be difficult. Have you found something out? Something new?"

"I've been to the police and I've been to the Community Service, so there will be a lot more people looking for Robbie."

"But have you learned anything more about where she is?"

I had to tell her the truth. "No, I haven't."

A sickly, stricken look crossed her face, whitening the corners of her downturned mouth and making her nostrils contract and her pale green eyes glitter. For a moment I thought she was going to pass out. When I moved to support her, she jerked away from me, folding her arms across her thin chest and hugging herself tightly. "I have this terrible feeling that she's dead," she said in an anguished voice. "Here." She grabbed her blouse and twisted it with her hand. "I'm afraid my daughter is dead."

"We have no proof of that," I said.

"She was with Bobby Caldwell!" she almost shouted at me. "Isn't that proof enough? He got her into terrible, terrible trouble. I'm sure of it."

"We don't know that," I said again.

"I don't think I could stand it," Mildred said. "To see Robbie . . . like the Caldwell boy." Her face had gone white and panicky.

71

I moved toward her and she backed away, knocking a glass ashtray off an end table and onto the carpet.

"Oh, my God!" she cried out and her hands fluttered about her face. "Oh, God, look at what you made me do!" She fell to her knees and cradled the ashtray to her breast. "Oh, God," she groaned.

"Mildred," I said gently. "For all we know, your daughter is in a shelter."

She looked up at me—her red eyes streaming with tears—and shook her head. Her face had that strained, saturated look of overexposure. The look of someone who's been out in merciless weather for far too long. She was on the edge of her own emotional limits and I had the feeling that if I didn't say or do something to sober her up she might break down completely.

"Wherever Robbie is," I heard myself say, "I'll find her and bring her home to you. I promise you, Mildred. I'll find her."

I bent down beside her and whispered, "It's going to be all right." Then I put my arms around her and held her. After a time, I took a handkerchief from my pocket and wiped off her face.

"I thought you didn't like me," she said with surprise.

"I don't dislike you," I said, trying to find a way to explain it—what I'd been feeling for two days. "It's this street. I grew up on a street like this. I know it too well."

"Why do you hate it?"

I helped her to her feet. She was still clutching the glass ashtray to her breast. I pulled it away and put it back on the end table.

"I don't hate it," I said. "I just don't agree with it."

She laughed weakly. "I don't think you're being honest."

72

"Perhaps not," I said. "Are you all right?"

She shook her head. "No, I feel awful."

"I'm sorry if what I said this morning—if it upset you."

"It's not you, Harry." She took a deep breath and said, "Maybe I'd better lie down for a bit."

"Do you want me to call anyone? A neighbor?"

"There's no one to call," she said simply. "If you'd stay here, just for a bit. Until I fell asleep?"

"All right. I wanted to look through Robbie's room again, anyway."

We turned to the stairs like an old married couple retiring for the night.

"I'm sorry I broke down," she said. "It won't happen again."

When we got to the bedroom, she pressed my arm. "Thanks," she said. "I'll be O.K. now. I just needed a shoulder to cry on, I guess. I'll be fine." She turned to the door, then looked back at me. "I don't think you disagree with it, Harry. The street and all this." She gestured about her. "I think you're disappointed in it. And that's a very different thing. You seem to be a man who is easily disappointed in people. You must have very high standards."

"For everyone but myself," I said with a laugh.

"No," she said earnestly. "I don't believe that. You're idealistic, which is what makes you such an odd man. As for me . . . I just want things to be the way they were. I just want my daughter back."

She stepped into the bedroom and closed the door behind her.

I spent an hour going through Robbie's things one more time. But I wasn't thinking about the girl as I looked over the books and the jewelry and the clothing. I was thinking about her mother, who was lying in a bed in the adjoining room, trying to make sense out of the jumbled materials of her own life—trying to piece it all back together, as if it were one of her china cups.

She'd come close to breaking down an hour before. So close it had worried me. I wasn't in the business of keeping other people sane. I knew that. But I'd acted as if I were, partly because the woman had needed reassurance, partly because I'd felt guilty for the way I'd treated her earlier that morning, and partly because it had been the only thing to do. It had been thoroughly unprofessional to pretend there was no reason to worry about Robbie's welfare. The whole business left me feeling vaguely conspiratorial, as if I'd committed myself to a scheme to keep Mildred from learning the truth about her daughter—not just the truth about what had happened to her, but the truth about what had happened to their relationship. Mildred only wanted things to be the same as they were; the truth was that they could never be the same again. Not after what had happened to Bobby Caldwell. Not after what she'd begun to discover about Robbie. And not after what Robbie had probably learned about herself.

10

I DIDN'T FIND ANYTHING NEW IN ROBBIE'S ROOM. I
spent a few minutes thumbing through the Gurdjieff and
the Rueben books. The one looked like it had barely been
opened; the other had been thoroughly read and under-
scored, as if Robbie had been prepping for an exam in sex
education. It would have been easy to make a good deal
out of that, if I hadn't dimly remembered my own adolescence and all those nights spent squinting over art books
and medical texts in my father's study. That was how I
picked up my sex education—ogling paintings by Rubens
and nude photographs of hebephrenics. It's no wonder
you're an odd man, Harry, I said to myself.

The hash pipe and the papers had been purchased at
The Head Shop in Mt. Adams. Thumbnail price tags
were still attached to each. There was no store label in
the T-shirt or on any of the other items. I put them all
back in the cardboard box, put the box in the closet, and
closed the sliding door. The house was still and sleepy,
save for the faint hum of the refrigerator in the kitchen.
I tiptoed past Mildred's bedroom and down the stairs.

Outside, everything was still and sleepy, too. The boys

had gone in from the playfield. And the street was deserted, except for a tall, gray-haired priest sweeping dust from the cobbled stairs leading to the school. I watched him for a moment—lean, black, intent—bent to his work as if the sweeping actually meant something, as if he wouldn't have to do the same thing again the next afternoon when the boys trudged in from the playfields. He finished with a flourish, tamping the broom stoutly on the stone then putting his hands to his hips with the air of a man well satisfied with what he'd done. He went inside and I turned back to the street, back to my job.

I walked up the sidewalk to the Rostow home. Past the plaster Negro with his wide-eyed, bedevilled look. And up to the paneled door. Madge Rostow answered my knock.

She had a plaid scarf on her head and a plaid apron on over her blouse and pants. Little taffy-colored curls had escaped from under the scarf and a big lock was dangling in the middle of her face. She blew it out of her eyes with an exhausted huff and smiled at me wearily.

"You caught me in the middle of house cleaning," she said. "Thursday is my day to sweep and dust."

"I just wanted to speak to Sylvia for a minute."

She nodded smartly—like a second lieutenant's salute. "Sure. Come in."

I walked into the living room and sat down on the edge of the couch. Madge went over to the staircase and shouted, "Syl?"

"What do you want?" the girl shouted back.

Madge Rostow flashed me an apologetic smile, then turned back to the staircase with something like vengeance in her eyes. "Get down here!" she commanded.

"Aw, Mom," the girl called out.

Madge turned back to me. "We read about Bobby Caldwell. My Lord, it's hard to believe that that could happen on this street. I mean, you usually read about those things happening in Covington or Milford or some godawful place. But on Eastlawn Drive!" She shook her head disbelievingly. "It didn't have anything to do with Robbie, did it? That would just be too horrible, if Robbie . . . Mildred must be a nervous wreck."

"She's in a pretty bad way," I said.

Madge Rostow pulled the scarf off of her head and her hair bobbed once, as if it were suspended on a heavy spring, then settled into a permanent wave. "I'm going to go talk to her," she said with concern. "I tried calling her earlier this morning, but the line was busy."

I started to tell her that Mildred was sleeping, then checked myself. Mildred needed the company and, besides, I wanted Sylvia to myself. The Rostow woman walked to the door just as her daughter came downstairs. The girl had a bottle of Coke in her left hand. When she saw me sitting there, she froze and looked beseechingly at her mother.

"Mom," she whined. "I don't want to talk to him."

"Don't be ridiculous," Madge Rostow said. "I'm going next door and if I come back and find out that you've been rude, I'm going to ground you for the week."

"Mom!" the girl cried.

But Madge was already out the door and down the walk.

Sylvia Rostow stared after her mother for a moment, then turned slowly back to me. She stood on the landing, pivoting on one bare foot—her right hand on the bannister, her left holding the Coke bottle. She had the same smug, arrogant look on her face that she'd had the day before. Only this time I thought I saw a bit of fear in her eyes. It made her whole posture look slightly unnatural, like the pose of a fourteen-year-old model trying to look all grown up. She stood on the landing for another couple of seconds, then sashayed into the living room. She was wearing blue denim overalls and a pink bib-collar blouse. She collapsed on one of the chairs, boosted the Coke to her mouth, and pretended to sip on it. But her eyes didn't leave my face.

"You read about Bobby, didn't you?" I said.

She nodded—the Coke still at her lips. She pulled the bottle away suddenly, with a smacking noise, and rubbed her round mouth. "I don't have to talk to you," she said with bravado. "I don't want to. And I don't have to."

"Do you know who did that to him, Sylvia? Who cut him up like that?"

"I told you," she said. "I don't want to talk about that."

"Would you rather talk to the police?" I asked.

Her plump round face went white. "What do you mean the police? What do I have to do with it?"

"You were a friend of Bobby's, weren't you? The police will want to talk to his friends."

She pulled herself up in the chair and tried to smile at me. "I wasn't his friend," she said almost gaily. "You've got the wrong idea, if you think I was his friend. Robbie was his friend. She's the one you should talk to."

"Only she's a little hard to find at the moment, Sylvia. You know that."

"So?" she said. "What am I—her keeper or something? Go talk to her, why don't you? And just leave me out of it."

"What are you frightened of, Sylvia?" I said. "What's scaring you?"

"Who said I was scared?" she said with a phoney laugh.

"I'm not scared. I just don't want to talk to you. O.K.?"

I shook my head and the smile came right off her face.

"Look," she said. "Just get out of my life, O.K.?"

"Not until you tell me what's frightening you."

"Nothing's frightening me!" she shouted and pounded so hard on the arms of the chair that a bit of Coke spouted out of the bottle. "Just quit saying that, O.K.?"

"Is it what happened to Bobby?" I said. "Is that what's bothering you? Did it have something to do with Robbie Segal?"

She bit her lip and looked longingly at the front door.

"Momma's not here right now, Sylvia," I said. "It's just you and me."

She whirled in the chair. "I don't want to talk about what happened to Bobby. Understand? I don't. O.K.?" She bit her lip again. "I don't know anything about it. So why don't you leave me alone."

"All right, Sylvia."

She made a small, satisfied face, as if she weren't quite sure she'd won out.

I got up from the couch and started for the door. She followed me with her eyes—the look of triumph growing bolder, less contained.

"I can't make any promises about the police, though," I said over my shoulder. "You'll have to talk to them."

"I don't believe you," she said cunningly.

"Believe what you want. But I'm telling you, I'm going to have to go to the police."

"Why?" she said sweetly. "Why do you have to do that? I told you I didn't know anything. Why do you have to go to the police?"

"Because I think you're lying," I said, staring at her coldly.

For a second I thought she was going to throw the

79

Coke bottle at me. Sylvia Rostow was a little girl so used to getting her own way that she thought she was invincible. And like most men and women who slide through life on charm alone, she was fully capable of murdering anyone who threatened her powers. "I hate you!" she said furiously. "You're a real bastard."

"All right, I'm a bastard. But if you don't want the police to come calling, you'll answer my questions."

She flung herself back in the chair and stared daggers at me. "I'm not going to talk about Robbie," she said through her teeth. "I don't know anything about Robbie."

"What about the Caldwell kid, then? Do you have any idea who might have done that to him?"

"I don't know," she said. "He hung around with some people at school . . ."

"What people?"

"I don't know," she said and tossed her head dramatically. "Greasers. Why don't you talk to them?"

"What are their names?"

"I don't know."

"C'mon, Sylvia," I said. "Give me a name."

"Hank Lemon," she spat out. "There. Satisfied?"

I wrote the name down in my notebook. "Where does he live?"

"On the other side of Eastlawn," she said. "Near Bobby."

She'd lost interest in the talk. I could see it in her face. Which probably meant that giving me Hank Lemon's name hadn't really cost her anything she wasn't fully prepared to give up. Whether there was more there—whether she actually suspected some connection between Bobby's death and Robbie's disappearance, or

80

whether she was just putting on a show—I couldn't tell. She liked being the center of attention. I knew that much. On the other hand, her fear of the police seemed genuine. But then most teenagers were afraid of the police. And most teenagers didn't like to snitch on their friends, either.

She tilted the Coke to her lips and drained it noisily. "I don't want to talk any more," she said, tossing the empty bottle on the rug. "Go on and tell the cops about me if you want to. My dad won't let anything happen to me."

She got up and walked across the room to the staircase. "Go on and tell them," she said over her shoulder. "See if I care."

I found an Anthony Lemon on Eastlawn in Madge Rostow's phone book. The address was just a couple of houses down from Pastor C. Caldwell's apartment. It would have been a short walk from the Rostow home. Only I didn't feel like walking it. Not after the previous night. So I stepped out to the street, got in the Pinto, and drove down the block—coasting by the big yellow apartment houses and their treeless yards—until I got to a small, red-brick four-family, with white siding on the upper story and a tiny cement stoop. There were two holly bushes planted on either side of the stoop and a pair of Pennsylvania Dutch planter boxes hanging from each of the lower-story windows. The only things growing in the muddy dirt of the planters were cigarette butts—a neat row of them, stubbed and half-buried in the soil.

I opened the storm door and stepped into a small tiled hall. There were two apartment doors on either side of the landing and a staircase opposite the door, leading up to the second-story apartments. Another stairway led to the basement. Someone was working on his car downstairs. I could hear an engine racing and the clatter of tools in a tool box.

I found Anthony Lemon's name on the mailbox—Apartment Two—and knocked on the right-hand door. A small, fat man in a white T-shirt and chino work pants answered my knock. The shirt was too small for him. It rode up his big, pendulous belly, leaving a pale layer of naked flesh hanging beneath it. The rest of Anthony Lemon was just as pale and fleshy as his beer gut. Fat, sweaty face, ringed at the neck with double chins. Curly black hair that looked wet to the touch. And a fat man's innocent blue eyes and bee-stung lips.

"Yeah?" he said gruffly. "What can I do for you?"

His breath smelled of beer. The apartment behind him of garlic and onions.

"I'm looking for Hank Lemon," I said.

"Downstairs," the man said and shut the door.

I turned to the stairway and the door opened again. The fat man rested one arm on the jamb and eyed me suspiciously.

"Who are you?" he said.

"My name is Stoner. I'm a private detective." I got my I.D. out of my wallet and showed it to him. "Are you Hank's father?"

"Yeah," he said slowly. "What of it?"

"I just want to ask the boy a few questions, Mr. Lemon. He isn't in any trouble."

"This have something to do with that Caldwell kid getting bumped off?"

I nodded.

"That was something, wasn't it?" the fat man said with vague enthusiasm. "Boy, that was something."

"Did you know Bobby Caldwell?" I asked him.

"Sure, I knew Bob. He was an O.K. kid. You can take it from me. Good head on his shoulders. Good with his hands, too. He would have made a damn fine mechanic. He and Hank . . . they worked on cars together." His face darkened suddenly. "You don't think my boy had something to do with the murder, do you?"

He didn't give me a chance to answer him. "You better not come around here making any trouble. I got a boy in the Marine Corps twice your size. You come around here making trouble for Hank—you're going to be plenty sorry."

"No trouble, Mr. Lemon," I said. "Just a few questions."

He eyed me again and jerked his head toward the basement door. "Downstairs, like I said."

I could feel him watching me all the way down to the first landing. "I'm keeping an eye on you," I heard him call out.

The basement walls were unpainted cement block, the floor unpainted concrete. I followed a row of light bulbs to the doors that led to the twin garages. A tall, skinny boy in workshirt and jeans was standing in one of the garages, working on a Plymouth. He had the motor running and the outside door open to vent exhaust.

He didn't see me at first—he was so engrossed in what he was doing. I had to walk up and tap him on the arm to get his attention.

He jerked his head up from under the Plymouth's hood and stared at me. "Man," he said over the roar of the engine. "You scared me."

83

He was a tall, swarthy sixteen year old, with dark brown eyes, very white teeth, and a steep straight nose that made him look vaguely like an Indian. The only feature he'd clearly inherited from his father was his black, curly hair. He reached inside the car and shut off the engine, then looked back at me.

"I said you scared me," he said again. His voice was high-pitched and boyish.

"Sorry," I said. "Are you Hank Lemon?"

He nodded.

"My name's Stoner. I'm a private detective."

He blinked once and grinned. "You're kidding?" he said. "An honest-to-God private detective?"

I showed him my I.D.

"Far out!" he said. "Well, what can I do for you, Mr. Stoner?"

"Sylvia Rostow gave me your name. She said you were a friend of Bobby Caldwell's."

Hank Lemon's big grin died so quickly and completely it was as if he'd never learned how to smile. "I don't really want to talk about that," he said somberly.

I searched his face, looking for a trace of the fear I'd seen in Sylvia Rostow's eyes. If it was there, I couldn't find it. Hank Lemon didn't look frightened—just sad and, I thought, a bit angry. The way anyone would look who'd lost a friend to senseless violence.

"I'd really appreciate it if you would talk about it, Hank," I said. "A girl's life could depend on it. A girl whom Bobby cared a great deal for."

"You mean Robbie, don't you?" he said.

"That's exactly who I mean."

The boy reached down and pulled a red rag from a tool chest sitting on the garage floor. He stared at me as he wiped off his hands. "You're working for her mother, aren't you?"

I told him yes.

"It's no wonder she's the way she is," he said after a moment. He threw the rag back into the box and kicked it shut. "What with her mother always bitching at her."

"What way is that?" I said.

He shrugged and looked a bit embarrassed. "A little spacey, I guess. Bob was taking care of her, though. I think she would have been all right, if this . . ." He sighed heavily.

"How was he taking care of her?" I asked him.

"He loved her, man," Hank Lemon said. "He looked after her. Man, he loved that chick."

"Do you think he would have helped her run away from home?"

"He would have helped her do anything," the boy said.

"She's been missing for five days, Hank," I told him.

"I didn't know that. I hadn't talked to Bob since last Friday."

"Did he say anything on Friday—anything that might explain what happened to Robbie or what happened to him?"

Hank Lemon shook his head. "He talked about cars and he talked about his music. That's all he ever talked about, except for Robbie. He said he'd written a couple of new songs. And he was hoping to get a gig this weekend to make enough money to finish up work on the Buick."

"Where did he play?" I said.

"He had some friends on the Hill. I never met them.

They'd play at small clubs, wedding receptions. That sort of thing."

I reached into my coat and took out the picture of Robbie and her two older friends. "Do you recognize the man or the woman?"

"No," he said.

"Could they be some of Bobby's musician friends?"

"I suppose. I told you I never met any of them. I'm just not into making music like Bob was. I don't hang around with that crowd. Some of them are just too spacey for me."

"How is that?"

He didn't want to spell it out. At least, he didn't want to spell it out to me—probably because I was the law. "Just spacey, man."

"You mean drugs, don't you?"

He stiffened up and said, "I didn't say that. You did. I don't know what all they were into, and I didn't want to know. That was their business, you know?"

"Do you have any idea why Bobby was murdered?"

He shook his head. "He was a good guy, mister. Easy going. Real laid back. All he wanted to do was play his music and work on his cars and love Robbie." Hank Lemon's swarthy face filled with grief. "I guess that was asking too much, huh?"

"I guess it was," I said heavily.

11

I SPENT THE REST OF THURSDAY AFTERNOON DRIVING through the green, hilly streets of Roselawn. The Lemon boy had given me the names and addresses of several other teenage boys—Bobby Caldwell's friends. One by one, I found them. In yellowstone apartments and red brick colonials, in ranch houses and stucco bungalows. Each of them told me the same things about Bobby— that he'd been a gentle, likeable, unambitious kid, with a passion for stock cars and music and Robbie Segal. His Robbie. That was the way they thought of her—as Bobby Caldwell's girl. He was taking care of her, they all said. He'd do anything for her. Anything.

And as the afternoon wore on toward sunset and all those young, shaken faces began to merge into a single, uncomprehending mask of grief, I realized that none of them could adequately explain what had happened to their friend. None of them had ever before experienced the violent death of one of their own. And if they'd already begun to turn him into a myth, into something as sweetly silly as his own songs—Bobby Caldwell, the boy who had lived for love—it was only because they didn't know any other way to talk about what had happened. They hadn't yet learned how to think about a death. But death is a quick study. And like sex, it carries its own vocabulary with it. In a matter of weeks, the words would come automatically and the event would shrink before them, until one day it wouldn't mean very much at all.

Of course, I'd sounded them out. On everything from the photographs to Bobby's musician friends. And heard nothing new. Not even about Robbie Segal, although by the time I'd started back to Clifton that fact had begun to intrigue me.

They didn't really seem to know very much about her, these gangly, red-faced, unreflective boys. She was a mystery to them—an aloof, lonely young girl whom Bobby, for some reason, had taken under his wing. Of course, most girls were a mystery to them at age sixteen. And they had been Bobby's friends rather than the girl's. But in spite of that, I ended up thinking there was something more to their confused looks and embarrassed silences than a normal teenager's uncertainty about the opposite sex. Something was wrong with Robbie Segal, that was the sense I got of it. They not only didn't understand her, they didn't like her, either. She was too strange. Too peculiar. A girl with a secret all her own.

No one said it outright. Perhaps out of loyalty to their dead friend. The closest they got to it were the code words they used to describe her—words like "cold," "spacey," and "far out." And all of them blamed Mildred for her peculiarities, as if it were self-evident that a teenager's problems were brought on by bad parenting. They were speaking for themselves, of course. But, in this case, I detected something hollow in the explanation, as if, in spite of their disenchantment with the world of fathers and mothers, even they couldn't quite make Robbie Segal fit the pattern. It "must have been" her parents was what they were really saying. Wasn't it always?

I didn't know. But I had my doubts. And not just about Mildred, who seemed to be as much her daughter's victim as her persecutor, although I knew perfectly well how hard it must have been for Robbie to live in that house. But then that house was no different than a hundred other houses on Canova and Elbrook and Section Road. Houses in which the boys I'd talked to lived. Grudgingly. Sometimes despairingly. But lived nonetheless. Robbie apparently didn't fit into their world any better than she'd fit into Mildred's. By the end of the day, as I drove back to the Delores through the blue velvet twilight, I'd begun to wonder where indeed she did fit —what that beautiful girl-child had run away to.

The boys I'd talked to would have answered, "To Bobby Caldwell." He'd been her protector and, almost certainly, her lover. She'd run away to be with him.

It was the simplest and, therefore, the most likely answer. She'd gone to a place where she could be with her lover. Perhaps to the house in the photograph—the house where Bobby and his musician friends gathered on the porch to jam and to smoke dope with the man in the beret. After talking to Hank Lemon, I'd begun to think that that man might be a musician, too. It helped to explain the look on his face—that severe, heavy-lidded, devilish stare, which was like a whispered threat or a kind of swagger. It was the look, I thought, of an overaged prodigy. The look of a man whose talents had dissolved into mere powers. It didn't take much imagination to spin out a scenario involving that man and Bobby and Robbie Segal. Together in that house with plenty of smoke and pills and time to kill. And sex in the air like a kind of spell. It didn't take much imagination to see what could have happened—how violence could have erupted. But then violent crimes seldom take much imagination to execute. Just a momentary weakening of conscience. A capitulation to impulse. Made all that much simpler in an environment where impulse was probably celebrated and encouraged. I could see it, all right. Right through to its bloody end.

And yet . . . and yet. Bobby Caldwell didn't seem like a completely satisfactory reason to me. Not for this one. Not for this beautiful girl with a secret. If I'd read Bobby's pals correctly, this one had wanted something more than a teenage boyfriend who wrote her pretty songs. This one had wanted something that even her friends couldn't figure out. Or so I thought. Maybe it was just wishful thinking. Maybe I wanted to make her into someone stronger and more buoyant than she really was —someone who could fly above and away from the world of Eastlawn Drive. Because secretly I liked the idea that the other kids didn't understand or approve of her. Secretly I felt a kinship to the girl I'd conjured up out of scrap and rumor and my own past. Secretly, I think, I wanted her to make her escape good—to disappear into an anonymous freedom, unhampered by Mildred or Bobby Caldwell or the man in the beret. Or by me.

Only I also knew that, in this world, the compass of experience always points away from the heart. That true north was always tougher, less satisfying, and more ordinary than any wish or hope. In this world, banality was

90

the rule, as drained and circumspect as a traffic fine. In this world, she was most likely sitting on that porch right now. Or buried under it.

It was almost dark by the time I got back to the Delores—the four-story U-shaped apartment building I'd lived in for at least an eon. I parked the Pinto in the tar lot and sat there for a moment, watching the last of the sunset bleed away into the firred hilltops. Outside the night air smelled strangely of lilac and automobile exhaust—the gas-station-in-the-countryside smell of spring in Cincinnati. I walked through the bouquet, past the budding dogwoods in the front yard and the leafy rosebushes, upstairs to my two-and-a-half room apartment.

I checked the answerphone as soon as I got inside. But there weren't any messages for me—not even from Mildred Segal. For a second, I toyed with the idea of calling her myself, to make sure she was holding up. I toyed with the idea, then let it go. At that moment, there wasn't anything I could do to make Mildred feel all right—except to tell her another lie. And I was too old for those kind of lies. Too old to promise anyone that I could make it better again. Not that she would have believed me, any more than she had believed me earlier that afternoon. She'd trusted the impulse behind what I'd said—the desire to help—but she hadn't believed the words. She'd had no reason to believe them. Besides, they conflicted with her own fantasies of guilt and retribution—with her feeling that the whole affair was a punishment visited upon her for her failures as a mother.

Mildred Segal was a shrewd, resourceful, surprisingly resilient woman who had run her life as she'd run her home—with stern, compulsive economy. For years, she'd taken comfort in the very nature of that economy —in the regular balancing of small risks and small gains. She'd lived the life of Eastlawn Drive more exactly than the best burgher could have done, putting her trust in the neat, clean display of her house and the careful ordering of her affections. It was a ledgerbook existence, kept in the neatest of hands; and it would probably have seen her through old age, if Robbie hadn't run away. That had thrown all her accounting off. That had made her economy seem like a kind of hubris—which, in fact, it was. And now she sat like a Greek in a tragedy, waiting for the gods to punish her for her way of life. And there was nothing I could say or do to alter that judgment. To be honest, I had thought she deserved it.

But part of me was beginning to feel a kinship to Mildred, too. Because part of me had been brought up to lead the same minimal kind of life—a life in which virtues and price tags were all jumbled together in the same box. I'd been fighting against that part since I'd come home from the war. Mostly successfully. Though, every now and then, I slipped. Who didn't slip? It was so much easier to live a life in which you're told the cost of every thought or act in advance, in which every idea is a received idea and every impulse is carefully weighed on the scale of public opinion before being acted on. With me, the tenets of Eastlawn Drive had been transmuted into a cranky pessimism; with Mildred, they'd become a conscious, unexceptioned creed. But we shared those tenets, nonetheless—I reacting against them, she believing in them. We were kin. Just as her daughter and I were akin in a different way.

It was odd, I thought, how easily I acquired families—

how quickly I discovered relations in the most unlikely people. Or perhaps that was just another side effect of my bachelorhood or of my job. Perhaps those "extended" families of mine were the only ones I'd ever have. At least, that was the way it was beginning to look as I got closer and closer to forty.

I sat on the Danish sofa in my living room, sipping a cold beer and pondering that depressing thought. I hadn't eaten since breakfast, and being hungry wasn't improving my mood. Eat and forget, I told myself. I flipped on the Globemaster, walked into my cubbyhole of a kitchen, and scrambled some eggs in a cast-iron skillet. I ate them right out of the pan, with a couple more beers for chasers. But I didn't really feel any better until Frances Shelley called at eight.

"I've run the check, Harry," she said.

"And?"

"Maybe we better talk about it in person. There's something else I want to tell you. Actually there's someone I want you to meet." But from the way she said it, she didn't sound as if she were looking forward to the rendezvous.

"If it has anything to do with your personal life, Fran . . ."

"It's all right," she said quickly. "I can handle this if you can. I'm going to introduce you to a friend of mine —a very good friend. She may be able to help you."

"All right," I said. "Where do we meet?"

"Do you know the City View Tavern in Mt. Adams?"

I said that I did.

"Then let's meet there. My friend lives right up the street."

"I'll meet you there in a half hour."

"And Harry?" she said in an unhappy voice. "My friend . . . she may want some money." She almost choked on the word. "Oh, Christ, I hope I'm doing the right thing."

"I'll bring some cash," I said. "And I'll be on my best behavior."

"All right," she said. "I'll see you in a half hour."

12

IT WAS A SHORT TRIP TO MT. ADAMS FROM THE DELORES —no more than fifteen minutes—and once I got above the expressway and into the park on the northeast side of the hill, I could smell the springtime in the air. The late April smells of wet earth and green, budding trees. The park was full of blue hyacinth and the grape-like clusters of flowering locust. I coasted past the reflecting pool beneath the Playhouse and up onto Ida, where the night sky was powdered with faint yellow light. Every evening, a blonde haze hung above the hill—the distillation of all the bar lights and restaurant lights and house lights on the hill's ritzy peak. Half-way down the slope, the money stopped and the lights began to go out.

I crossed the Ida Street viaduct, skirting the bright St. Gregory and Celestial tenderloins, and coasted down Monastery into the dark hinterlands. Oregon ran east off Monastery—a narrow, cobbled, gaslit street, heavily forested on the hillside and lined, on the city side, with boxy, two-story, frame-and-tar board apartment houses. A few of the buildings had widow's walks on their flat tin roofs and black decorative shutters on their facades; but for the most part, they were thoroughly run-down homes—poor cousins to the A-frames and high-rises on the crest of Mt. Adams.

I found a parking spot on the hill side of the street, beneath a budding mulberry tree, locked the Pinto, and walked down the block to the City View Tavern. I hadn't been near the City View since I was a college kid, when the combination of cheap beer, local color, and quaint surroundings had seemed irresistible. Twenty years later, the place looked exactly like what it was—a storefront bar on a run-down street. The inside hadn't changed much since my college days: small paneled tap room, decorated with Kiwanis posters and framed photographs of the inclined railroad that used to run past the bar on its way up to Celestial Street; round metal tables with cork tops that smelled vaguely of beer and of disinfectant; small, polished wooden bar, behind which rows of whiskey bottles glowed in the overhead light; and, through the rear door, an open-air deck overlooking the city, with its own complement of tables and festoons of Christmas tree lights winking steadily through the night.

It wasn't a busy evening at the City View. A couple of old men in light jackets and rayon pants were sitting on the bar stools, staring into their shot glasses. And a plump teenage girl with a pugnacious face was coaxing music out of a pinball machine on the side wall. I ordered a beer from the bartender and carried it through the rear door, out onto the terrace.

Frances Shelley was sitting with a young blonde girl at one of the tables. For a brief second, in the dim terrace light, I cherished the foolish hope that the girl was Robbie Segal. But as I walked up to her, I realized that the only thing that she and Robbie had in common was blonde hair; and even that proved to be an illusion, because this one's hair was peroxided. It covered either side of her thin face in curly muffs, like a poodle's ears.

When Frances reached over to brush some of the hair from the girl's cheek, the blonde shook her head and growled, "Cut it out, Fran!" in a husky, unpleasant voice. Frances dropped her hand immediately and glanced at me, as if she'd hoped I hadn't noticed what had happened. The girl stared at me, too.

"Harry," Frances said in a weak voice, "This is my friend, Sophie." She turned to Sophie, who was still giving me the evil eye, and said, "Sophie, this is Harry Stoner. A good friend."

I sat down at the table and, for a moment, none of us said a thing. After a while, Sophie unfastened her eyes from my face and looked off into the night.

Frances was watching her closely, as if she were taking her cue from what Sophie did and said. She was watching her with her heart in her eyes; and as always happens when you show your heart, you show all—what you love and what you fear.

"You see why I was nervous?" she said to me with a strained laugh and glanced quickly at Sophie.

"What the hell are you apologizing to him for?" the girl said, without turning her head. "And quit ogling me. You make me nervous."

"I'm sorry," Frances said.

"Cut it out, Fran," Sophie said again. "We've got nothing to be ashamed of."

Frances laughed unhappily. "For some reason, it doesn't feel that way."

"*He's* the reason," Sophie said. "Can't you see that?"

"I haven't said a word," I said.

The girl turned on me with the quickness of a big, prowling cat. "You don't have to say anything. In fact, the less you say, the better." She stared at Frances. "Where's the money you talked about, Fran? Let's get this over with."

"Sophie knows the name of the woman in that photograph you showed me," Frances explained.

"It'll cost you a hundred dollars," Sophie said smugly.

"All right," I said. "Who is she?"

"I'll get to it." The girl reached down beside her and pulled a pack of cigarettes out of a canvas bag. She tapped a cigarette into her hand, lifted it to her mouth, and looked at Fran. "Light me," she said coldly.

Frances snapped open a lighter and lit her lover's cigarette. Sophie puckered her lips and let the smoke dribble out of her mouth like a pale, white fluid. Then she licked her upper lip with the tip of her tongue and laughed hoarsely.

I was beginning to feel sorry for Frances. A one-sided relationship isn't much fun no matter who's involved in it. A politicized relationship is even worse. And this one looked like it was bound to end in heartbreak.

Sophie reached across the table and clicked the lighter shut. "You'll burn yourself, sweetie," she said with a sort of honeyed malice.

Frances ducked her head in embarrassment.

"About the woman?" I said.

Sophie passed her thumb across the tip of her cigarette, knocking the dead ash into a glass ashtray sitting on the table. "The money first," she said.

I took my wallet out of my coat and handed her four twenties and two tens. She plucked them delicately from my fingers, as if she were trying to avoid touching my flesh. "Her name's Irene Croft," she said, as she folded the bills and stuck them in her bag.

"No relation to *the* Crofts?" I said lightly. *The* Crofts were one of the first families of the city. Like *the* Tafts or *the* Scripps or *the* Procters of Procter and Gamble.

"I kind of doubt it," Sophie said wryly. "It would be pretty funny, if she were."

"How so?"

"She's kinky, that's why."

"And what does that mean?"

Sophie smiled wickedly. "She used to pay me money to have sex with her on the phone. Real dirty sex. She'd tell me what to do and then I'd tell her what to do. It usually lasted a couple of hours. Lots of heavy breathing. That kind of kinky."

Frances flushed and stood up. "That was a lousy thing to say in front of me," she said bitterly and ran across the terrace to the bar. Through the picture window I watched her go into the lady's room.

"Maybe you better go after her," I said to Sophie.

"Maybe you better mind your own fucking business," she said in an ugly voice. "Fran knows the way things are." She took a deep drag off her cigarette and flipped the butt over the terrace wall. "She's got a lot of growing up to do, that's all. She was divorced a couple of years ago and she's still into that desperate married mentality. She still wants to belong to someone—wants to be their property. I'm nobody's property. And I'm sure as hell not going to take someone else on. Especially someone who hasn't got her shit half-together."

She was something, Sophie was. A truly ugly character who lived by sexual whim and would probably die by it. I just hoped she didn't take my friend with her.

"About Irene Croft?" I said. "What else can you tell me?"

She shrugged. "She used to come to the club a lot— practically a charter member. But I don't see her much any more. I think she might have straightened out a little, because I caught a glimpse of her a few weeks ago cruising Fourth Street with a leather boy. Irene digs leather. Definitely not my bag."

Sophie looked up as Fran walked back to the table. Her eyes had a red, scrubbed look behind her glasses and her cheeks were flushed. She stared at Sophie and said, "I think we better go."

"One last question," I said. "Do you know where Irene Croft lives?"

Sophie picked up her bag and slung it over her shoulder. "In the Highland House." She started to put her arm through Frances's arm, and Frances pulled away. Sophie laughed lightly and sauntered toward the terrace door.

Frances scowled after her, then turned to me. I could tell what was coming from the look on her face. She'd been humiliated and I'd witnessed it. Perhaps she felt I'd been the cause of it. In any case, she was searching for someone other than Sophie to blame.

"I don't think we'll be seeing much of each other for a while, Harry."

"If that's the way you want it, Frances."

"That's the way I want it." She started to follow Sophie out the door, then looked back at me. "Sophie's just a little wild, that's all. But then she isn't very old. She hasn't seen a lot of life. And she just doesn't know how badly she can hurt me."

I said, "I think she knows exactly how to hurt you, Frances. I think she's good at it."

"Oh, for chrissake, Harry!" Frances cried. "Don't put that trip on me now. I don't need that trip. It's been a bad enough evening as it is."

"I'm sorry," I said. "I shouldn't have said it."

"Anyway, she's not always like that. She can be very sweet."

"If you say so, Frances."

"Oh, Harry," she said.

For a second we just looked at each other across the terrace.

"I gotta go," she finally said.

"If you ever need to talk about it, Frances . . ."

"You're the one I'll come to," she said. "By the way, I ran that check for you and didn't turn anything up. *Your* girlfriend isn't at a shelter, if that's any help."

"You've been a big help."

She nodded and walked into the tap room. Through the window I saw her exchange a few words with Sophie. Then they joined arms and walked out of the bar.

13

THERE WAS A COLD WIND RUNNING DOWN THE STREET when I stepped back out into the night. It shook the branches of the mulberry trees on the hill and whistled in the downspouts of the bleek boxy houses. I pulled my sports coat shut and, shoulders hunched, walked up Oregon to my car.

Once inside, I sat for a moment, thinking about Frances. The fact that she was a lesbian hadn't bothered me. Or only a little. It was her lover, Sophie, who made me sick at heart. It just didn't seem fair that someone as vulnerable as Frances should end up with someone like Sophie for a lover. Only, fair or not, that was what usually happened. It was just too damn easy to find someone with all the answers—someone so self-involved that he or she didn't care whether or not they were the right answer for you. Which made me think of Robbie Segal.

I started up the Pinto and circled down to Baum Street —a stretch of concrete so run down that even a Mt. Adams realtor couldn't find a way to dress it up—then back up Monastery to Celestial, at the top of the hill. I'd thought I was going to sidestep the bright, hazy lights that evening. But the Highland House was right in the middle of them—a huge steel high-rise on the crest of the hill, with its own barber shop and restaurants and saunas, like a little piece of Miami Beach on the banks of the Ohio. It was where the woman named Irene Croft lived. And, at that moment, Irene Croft was my only lead.

I parked in the guest lot across from the apartment house and stood there for a minute, with the wind riffling my hair, studying that huge rectangular monolith, full of picture windows and railed cement porches and curtain-filtered lamplight. There was only one way in—past a doorman in red livery, posted beneath a canopied entry-way at the foot of the building. And the doorman wouldn't buzz me through to the elevator room until he'd checked with Irene Croft, who wasn't about to let a private detective named Stoner come up for a chat. So I couldn't get directly into the apartment house, but I could go into the Celestial—the posh, glassed-in restaurant that occupied most of the ground floor of the high-rise. Then I could wait in the Celestial lobby, across from the elevator room, until a Highland House resident came downstairs for a late night stroll. And when he'd unlocked the inner door that led to the elevators, I'd manage to slip up to Irene Croft's apartment.

I was thinking about how to get her apartment number as I walked up to the doorman—an elderly black man with a face like a rubber mask.

"Cold night," I said.

He smiled pleasantly. "Too cold for April. Are you for the restaurant or the apartments, sir?"

"A little of each," I told him. "I'm supposed to meet one of your tenants for a drink. Her name's Croft."

The black man cracked a broad grin. "Miss Irene," he said, as if he'd raised her from a pup. "You want me to give her a buzz?"

"No," I said. "She said she'd meet me in the bar. If she isn't there, I'll take you up on your offer."

"No need to come back out in the cold again," he said. "There's a house phone in the lobby."

"Well, to be honest, I don't remember her apartment number."

"She's 2201," he said.

"High up."

"'Bout as high as you can get. Man, that's the penthouse."

"I'll be damned," I said.

I walked past him into the restaurant lobby—a dark ante-room with red flock walls and gilt trim and a couple of plush chairs for furnishing. Through the portal on the far wall, I could see a maitre d' sitting at a purser's desk, bent over his guest list like a conductor studying a score. Beyond him, the dining room shimmered with crystal and silver and snow-flake linen. It was too late for the dinner crowd—nine-thirty by my watch. But there was still a faint drone of table talk coming from inside the room. The high-pitched, vital sounds of men and women at play. I tucked myself away in a corner—on one of the upholstered chairs—and kept an eye on the plate glass doors leading to the elevators.

A few couples sauntered past me out of the restaurant. The men in business suits, looking flushed and pompous as only the well-fed can look. The women in evening gowns, leaning on their men with laughter in their eyes. I sat there like an unbidden guest, watching them come and go. And watching the inner door. And around ten

104

o'clock, the elevators clicked open and I got to my feet. A plump blonde woman in a tartan plaid poncho stepped out and walked to the inner door. She was leading a miniature poodle by a leash. The woman fumbled with her key, trying to keep the dog in line with her free hand. But he was capering around like a lunatic, making little leaps at the plate glass door and humping her leg furiously.

She finally managed to open the lock. And I held the door open for her as she came out.

"Bless you," she said with distress.

Then the dog broke into a run—its black nails scrabbling across the tile floor—and the woman flew after it, like someone blown away by a sudden wind. I slipped through the door and walked over to the bank of elevators. A minute later, I was on the twenty-second floor.

It wasn't until I actually walked up to the wood-paneled door of Irene Croft's apartment that I began to wonder what I was doing there. It had occurred to me that I had only the vaguest idea who the woman was and nothing but the photograph to connect her with Robbie Segal. And that wasn't much to go on. Her sex life, as sordid as it apparently was, didn't interest me, except as it might have involved Robbie. And whether she was one of *the* Crofts, which seemed more likely given her penthouse in Mt. Adams, was none of my concern, either. Every family has its black sheep, even the ultrarich, ultraconservative ones. The Crofts just had a doozie, that was all. I decided before I knocked that all I was really interested in was the man in the beret. If I could wheedle his name and address out of Irene Croft, I'd leave her to her obscene phone calls and her leather boys.

It wasn't a very specific plan of action, but it was the best I could come up with. I went ahead and knocked.

To my surprise, Irene Croft herself answered a few seconds later. She was taller than I'd expected from the photograph and boyishly thin. Tiny breasts, slender hips. She wore a black shirt with western piping and black leather pants with a silver belt through the loops.

"Yes," she said. Her voice was as mellow and vibrant as a plucked guitar string. "Who are you?"

"My name is Stoner," I said, and, unable to think of anything better to say, added: "I'm a friend of Robbie Segal's."

"Oh, yes?" the woman said with enough curiosity in her voice to make me think that she recognized the name. "What do you want?"

"Just to talk to you for a few minutes—about Robbie. She's been missing for several days and we're worried about her."

"You're a friend of the family's?"

"Yes."

The woman looked me over for a second. She had the blackest eyes I'd ever seen—almost all pupil with just a hint of dark blue iris at the circumference. The rest of her face seemed ridiculously ordinary by comparison. Thin lips, off-white teeth, pug nose, square jaw, short gray hair. She would have looked like a tall, skinny Dorothy Parker, if it hadn't been for those eyes. They gave her an inert, fathomless stare—like a doll's dead glass gaze.

"Who sent you to me?" she said mildly, as if it hardly mattered.

"If I could come in for a minute . . . ?"

She pulled the door open and stepped aside. "Certainly."

The entry hall ran behind a huge sunken living room, then continued back to the unlit rooms at the rear of the penthouse. Irene Croft led me down a short stairway to the living room and pointed to a Z-shaped chair. I sat down and took a quick look around me. The entire west wall was plate glass, and the city glowed behind it as if it were a piece of incandescent sculpture designed for that room alone. It was the most breathtaking view of Cincinnati I had ever seen. And it so absorbed me that, for a moment, I didn't notice that the other walls were hung with remarkable paintings. Picassos, Braques, Cezannes. Giacomettis on the creamy enameled tables. What looked like Moores in the corners. Even the furniture was special—sleek, Italian modern pieces in windswept shades of blue. The only light in the room—in the whole apartment, for that matter—came from the picture window and from the tiny white spots trained on the various artifacts. It made me feel as if I were sitting, after hours, in a museum. A vaguely privileged and slightly uneasy feeling. But then great wealth generally has that effect on me.

"You like my living room?" the woman said with a tickle of pride in her mellow voice.

"Very much. It's beautiful," I said, although I was really thinking about the distance between it and the Rostow's living room.

"I've tried to make it as beautiful as I could. If I have to live in this city, I can at least surround myself with beautiful things."

"You don't like Cincinnati?"

"Only the people who live in it," she said with a mild laugh. "But I'd decorate my rooms like this no matter where I lived. Collecting fine art is one of my weaknesses."

"That's an odd way to put it."

"I'm an odd woman." She laughed, exposing her tiny, off-white teeth. "You haven't come to rob me, have you, Mr. . . .? I don't believe I caught your name."

She said it so casually that it shook me—as if she were used to being vandalized, as if she expected it. But then if what Sophie had told me were true, she'd probably had her share of expensive, unreliable friends. "My name is Harry Stoner. And I've come to ask you a few questions about Robbie Segal."

"And how did you get up here, Mr. Harry Stoner?" she said in that same blasé tone of voice.

"I sneaked in," I told her.

She laughed again. "So enterprising and so handsome. What an unusual combination."

She sat down on one of the blue Italian sofas and tented her hands at her lips. She would have looked quite at home, if it weren't for her eyes. Those eyes would never look at home—no matter what city she lived in.

"I asked you a question a few minutes ago and you haven't answered me yet," she said from behind her tented fingers. "Who sent you here?"

I reached into my coat pocket and pulled out the snapshot of her and Robbie and the man in the beret. I passed it over to her, and she held it up to the window—to catch the city light.

"Not a very flattering likeness," she said softly. "Have you talked to Theo, too?"

I didn't even have to think about it. I said, "Not yet."

She gazed out the window at the winking lights. "He's a very great artist, you know," she said with a tremor in her voice. The sudden depth of feeling was surprising, given the cynical way she'd talked about everything else —including the possibility of being robbed. She must have heard it herself, because she straightened up in her chair and crossed her legs, as if showing her feelings were just another kind of bad posture. "He's one of the finest jazz guitarists this city has ever produced. One of the finest in the country." She said it flatly, like a tour guide reading from a Baedecker.

"I guess I'll have to hear him play some time."

"You must," she said. But her voice had shifted again —back into its cynical, blasé mode. "You really must, Mr. Stoner."

"Where does he play?"

She smiled knowingly, as if I'd suddenly begun to speak her idiom. "You don't know who Theo is, do you?"

"Just the name."

"Don't try to con me, Mr. Stoner. I've been conned by the best. You didn't know his name until I mentioned it a moment ago."

There was no sense in lying, because I figured she was right. A woman with her tastes *had* been conned by the best. Or the worst. I told her the truth. "No, I didn't."

"It doesn't matter," she said with a toss of her head. "Everyone lies. Theo Clinger plays in Mt. Adams. At The Pentangle Club in Hill Street. There's no reason you shouldn't know that."

"Is that where the photo was taken? At The Pentangle Club?"

"Why do you want to know?" she said curiously, as if she were anticipating another lie.

"I told you. Robbie's run away and we're worried about her."

"We?"

"Her mother," I said.

I pulled my wallet out of my coat, slipped the photostat of my license out, and handed it to her.

"My, my, my," she said with just a touch of resentment in her voice. She handed the license and the photograph back to me. "Your nose is going to grow two inches, Mr. Stoner, for all the little fibs you've told me. I have nothing to hide. Why didn't you tell me you were a detective right away?"

"Some people don't like talking to detectives," I said.

"Some people?" she said. "Or this particular person?"

"I came to you to talk about Robbie. Nothing more. At the moment you're the only lead I have. You and that photograph."

"Well, she's not here. I can assure you of that. And as far as I know she's not with Theo, either. To be uncharacteristically honest with you, I met her only twice. Once on the occasion that the picture was taken. And once at The Pentangle. Both times she seemed a sweet, intelligent young thing. Stunningly attractive, although I don't think she realized it. She seemed preoccupied with her mother. Life was apparently too restrictive at home." She glanced out the window again and said, "I could certainly sympathize with that. She was with a boy on both occasions. I don't remember his name, although I'm sure that Theo would. He played the guitar and Theo seemed to think he had real talent. I remember that the young man seemed very attached to Robbie."

"And how did she behave toward him?" I asked.

"Quite lovingly, I would say. But then I'm no expert on love, Mr. Stoner, as you may have heard. I had the feeling that she was more mature than he was, despite their difference in age. She seemed quite taken with the people she met at The Pentangle. The boy seemed a little jealous of that. But then I was a little jealous of him. If I were you I'd be looking for that boy. Robbie's probably with him."

"I hope not," I said. "The boy's name is Bobby Caldwell and he was murdered yesterday."

"Good God!" the woman said and put her hand to her mouth. "I see now why you came to me. You must be very worried about Robbie."

"Worried enough," I said with a sigh. "You're sure that she didn't run to Theo?"

"Positive," she said. "I was with him yesterday. Besides, he has a family of his own to look after." She made a strange face, but I didn't know what to make of it.

"Irene?" someone called from behind us.

I jerked around in my chair and the woman jumped to her feet with a furious look. The voice came from the entryway. A naked boy was standing on the stairs leading down to the living room. He was eyeing us with a sort of vain insouciance—one hand cocked on his hip and the other resting on the bannister. He was about eighteen or nineteen, with hair the color of gun metal and a thin, cold, copper-colored face as pretty as a brand new penny. He was tanned from head to foot and built like a weight lifter.

"I told you to stay away," the woman said through her teeth.

"You tell me a lot of things," the boy said and ambled into the room. He sat down on one of the chairs and stared at us with a pleased, naughty look—like a kid who's just gotten away with murder. "Who's the dude?" he said, nodding toward me.

Irene Croft sat back down and shook her head

111

woefully. There was anger on her face. But it was mixed with a number of other feelings. A touch of pride, I thought, as if in spite of it all she couldn't help admiring the kid's bravado. And a bit of laughter at my expense and at the expense of all the other straight arrows in the city. And something else. Something that brought her dead eyes to life for the first time since I'd met her. Something that filled them with fire and cunning. Something, I thought, very much like lust.

"Rudy, meet Mr. Stoner." She turned to me and said, "This is Rudy—my pet."

I nodded to the boy and he grinned foolishly.

Irene Croft got out of her chair and walked over to where the boy was sitting, and knelt down in front of him. "I think you better leave now, Mr. Stoner," she said, staring at the boy's body. "Unless you want to join us."

"I'll take a rain check."

"Then I hope you won't mind if I don't show you out."

"I don't mind."

I got up and walked to the door. I looked back once from the landing. Rudy had his legs draped over the arms of the chair and Irene Croft's head was buried between them.

14

MAYBE IT WAS THE AFTERSHOCK OF HAVING MET A cultivated monster like Irene Croft, but I felt buoyant and alert as I walked back to the car. I was on to something. For the first time in a couple of days. Whether that something would lead me to Robbie Segal, I didn't know. Irene Croft had assured me that it wouldn't. But then Irene Croft was a fundamentally dishonest woman. If she had told me the truth about Robbie, I figured she'd done it for a reason that had nothing to do with concern for the girl's safety. She'd done it to help herself, because, at bottom, that was the only reason she really understood.

I got in the car and drove up to Hill Street. A few stragglers were staggering along the sidewalks—drunk and melancholy, weaving lonely patterns through the April night. Most of the buildings were closed up—the houses, the shops, the groceries. But here and there, a bar door stood open and through it came a sudden roar of life—guitars, drum sets, voices, all mixed together with the clanging of pinball machines and the tinkling of glass. A hundred feet farther on, the street would go quiet again, except for the muttering drunks and the occasional sightseers, still wandering arm in arm up the steep, windy sidewalks.

I found The Pentangle Club on Hill, where it intersected St. Gregory. It was located on the first floor of a made-over, three-story Victorian, with twin gables and a long front porch. A sign hanging from the porch roof read *Pentangle*. There was a placard set up beneath it, with the names of the artists who were performing there that night. Theo Clinger wasn't among them. I decided to go inside anyway—just to nose around.

I parked the Pinto on St. Gregory and walked up to the corner of Hill. From the outside, The Pentangle Club seemed very different than the raucous bars farther up the street. For one thing, there was no roar coming out the open door. Just the sweet, recorded sound of a woman's voice—Billie Holiday, I thought—singing wistfully of lost love. The wind blew her voice out to me, swallowed it up in a sudden gust, then brought it floating back again, as if it weren't a record I was hearing but a real woman, singing softly through a window, unaware she was being listened to.

Oh why, oh why is love so strange?
Why you want me? Why you come back again?
You say you leave me, but you never let go.
You say you love me, but you hurt me so.

The woman's voice—gravelly, sweet, resigned—was shrewd and laconic. She sang the lyrics as if she were thinking them out as she went along, as if she were discovering for the last time that love was strange.

I listened to her until the song was over, then stepped onto the porch. It didn't look at all like the porch in the

114

photograph. In fact, this one was more of a veranda—a broad, plank deck with a pitched roof overhead. I walked across it into The Pentangle.

A teenage girl was sitting on a rocking chair just inside the door. She was dressed like one of the Pointer Sisters, in a tight, print, hand-me-down dress, black high-heeled shoes, and silk stockings with a dark seam down the back of each leg. She had a black straw hat cocked on her head with a long ostrich feather stuck in the band. She smiled at me and I smiled back.

"Who was that singing just now?" I asked her.

"That was Billie Holiday," she said. "Did you like her?"

"I have for years," I said.

"Lady Day," she said blissfully.

She was a pretty, blonde kid with very pale lashes and brows and very pale skin. Her emerald eyes and pink lips were the only spots of color in her face. I figured she was no more than eighteen or nineteen. But I could have been wrong. From the way she'd outfitted herself, she seemed to have a well-developed sense of style; and that wasn't something she could have picked up overnight.

"I'd show you to a table," she said. "But we're getting ready to close."

"Do I have time for a beer?"

"Sure. Tell Joey it's on the house."

"Why so generous?" I said.

"I don't know," she said with a giddy laugh. "Because you like Billie Holiday."

"Thanks," I said to her.

The bar was on the far side of the room. Tables and chairs were set up between it and a small, spotlit stage near the door. The stage was empty, but a few kids were

115

still sitting there staring at it with devotion, as if it might suddenly come to life and make music again. I wondered who'd been playing there that night.

I asked the bartender and he said, "Jim Tuttle. Jazz sax. He's great, man. Great."

The jukebox started to play—Charlie Parker. I leaned up against the bar rail and looked out across the room.

"We had coffee houses in my day," I said to the bartender—a young, red-headed giant with razor-burned cheeks, a sparse red moustache, and pale blue eyes.

"Great, man," he said.

I laughed and turned back to him. "How about giving me a Scotch? Johnny Walker Red Label. Straight up."

He turned to the liquor shelf and picked up a quart bottle with a chrome spout. "Can't see how you drink this stuff," he said flipping the Scotch into a shot glass. "Tastes like medicine to me."

"Give me my medicine," I said.

He smiled and set the glass in front of me, as daintily as if he were building a model ship. He pulled a bar rag from a metal loop and began to polish glasses.

"Coffee house, huh?" he said as he worked.

"Well, that's what we called them. But all I remember drinking is tea. We were just hippies imitating the beatniks."

"Everybody's got to believe in something," he said. "You had Woodstock and we got Iggy Pop."

"Here's to Iggy Pop," I said. "And all that he stands for."

I downed the Scotch and put the glass on the bar. "One more."

He poured me another Scotch. I picked up the glass. "Who are we drinking to this time?"

"To peace and love," he said with a grin.

"To peace and love." I swallowed half of it and began to feel good. "Who's the girl by the door?" I asked him.

"Her name's Grace."

"She work here?"

"On weekends," the boy said. "Mostly she hangs out. She's a jazz freak. Goes to CCM. Or used to. She actually has a pretty nice voice. She sings here when The Count plays."

"Who's The Count?"

He looked at me with surprise. "You don't know who The Count is, man? The Count is God."

"That's a hard act to book," I said.

He laughed. "You don't know the half of it."

"When's The Count playing again?"

"Theo?" he said. "Next Monday, I think."

I took another sip of the whiskey and said, "Theo? I thought you called him The Count."

"Oh, that's just bullshit. He calls himself the Lost Prince, too. His real name is Theo Clinger. And he's a helluva musician. A little weird, but first class. Maybe the best in the city."

"What's he play?"

"He *plays* the guitar," the bartender said in a hip voice. "But you better get here early if you're thinking about coming to hear him."

"He's got a big following?" I said.

The boy said, "Following is the word. Theo's practically got a family of worshippers." He said it a little sourly, as if he preferred to worship somewhere else.

"Is she part of his family?" I nodded toward Grace.

"A charter member. She lives with him, but then a lot of the chicks do."

I gave him a surprised look, although I wasn't very surprised.

"Oh, yeah," he said coolly. "The Count loves the little girls. And the little boys, too, from what I hear. He's got a *devoted* following. And they do what he says."

His voice had soured again. It made me wonder if he'd lost a little girl of his own to The Count's troupe. It also made me wonder about Robbie Segal. I took the photograph out of my pocket and tossed it on the bar.

The boy's face darkened and something in his eyes—some spark of amusement that had kept our conversation loose and amiable—blew right out. "You're a cop, aren't you," he said. "Yeah, you're a cop. I guess I should have known that." He slapped the wet towel against the bar, as if he were flogging himself for his stupidity.

"I used to be a cop," I said. "I used to be a hippie, too."

"Just exactly what are you now, mister?" he said, staring at me coldly.

"Now, I'm a private detective, looking for the girl in this picture. She's a runaway and her mother wants her back."

He swiveled the picture around with one finger and eyed it casually. "I don't want any trouble with the cops," he said. "We're on probation with the State Board right now."

"There won't be any trouble. I just want to find the girl."

He nodded, but he didn't look as if he believed me. "I don't think I've seen her before."

"Think again, Joey."

He looked up at me quickly. "How did you know my name?"

"Grace told me."

118

"Well, why don't you take your photograph and your Scotch and go talk to Grace? I never saw this girl before in my life." He turned to the shelves of liquor bottles and began dusting off their caps. Somewhere along the line he'd been pushed too hard by someone in blue serge, and he wasn't going to be pushed again. It irked me a little that he'd automatically lumped me together with whoever that was. To be honest, it irked me that he lumped all cops together in the same bin.

I downed the rest of the Scotch and laid a ten-dollar bill on the bar. "Keep it," I said to him.

"You *keep* it," he said under his breath. "And keep the fuck out of my bar. I don't like cops."

"I don't like bartenders," I said.

He whirled around and planted his hands on the mahogany rail. "You want to make something out of it?"

"Just a point," I said. "Cop or bartender—it's only a job."

"Well, I don't like your job," he said between his teeth.

I picked up the photograph and the money, stuck them in my coat pocket, and walked over to the front door. Grace had apparently been watching us from where she was sitting.

"What happened?" she said as I came up to her.

"Joey decided that he didn't like my job," I said with disgust. I was angry, and I knew that I shouldn't have been. Not with a twenty-three-year-old kid with a red moustache and a chip on his shoulder. Only it had been a long day; and I was beginning to feel the weariness inside me. It and the liquor and the lost girl. The booze had killed off the remainder of that buoyancy I'd been feeling, and now I just wanted to go home.

"What job is that?" she said curiously.

119

"I'm a private detective," I said. "Want to make something out of it?"

She grinned and I found myself smiling back at her.

"A private detective? I don't think I've ever met one of those before."

"Well, now you have."

As I started through the door, she picked up a black straw purse and followed me out.

"Where do you think you're going?" I asked her.

"With you."

"Why in the world would you want to do that?"

She thought it over as we stepped onto the porch. "Because you're the first private detective I've ever met who liked Billie Holiday."

15

THE WIND WHIPPED GRACE'S DRESS ABOUT HER LEGS AS
we walked up St. Gregory to where I'd parked the Pinto.
Out on the river a barge horn sounded one long, melancholy blast. The girl hooted back at it in a graceful, jazzy
soprano, pirouetted on her high heels, and flapped her
long arms like a water bird taking flight. She came back
to earth with a carefree laugh, planting a hand on her hat
and looping the other through my arm.

When we reached the car, I took a critical look at her.
She stared back at me with a loose, gum-cracking grin—
one leg shifted forward and bent at the knee, one hand
planted on her bony hip. In that long-sleeved, high-
necked print dress, she looked a little like a tough, brassy
broad from a forties melodrama. Of course that was the
way she'd wanted to look. But even though she'd dressed
the part to a tee, her face wasn't right. It should have
been fleshier, less chalky and delicate. She should have
had more meat on her bones, too. She looked tough, all
right, and cocksure, but she just didn't look full grown.
If she'd been five years older, she would have been tacky
and pathetic. As it was, she baffled me. I didn't know why

she'd picked me up. Or what in the world I was going to do with her later that night. But, somewhere in the back of my mind, I was thinking that she belonged to Theo Clinger's circle and that that was reason enough to play along.

"It's cold," she said, hugging her shoulders through the thin dress.

"I'll turn on the heater in the car."

We got in and I experienced another awkward moment, listening to her silk stockings rustle.

"How old are you?" I said as I started the engine.

"Old enough," she said drily. "I'm well past the jail bait stage, if that's what you're worried about." She tucked her legs underneath her, turned in the car seat, and gave me an amused look. "What are you worried about? You're worried about something."

I flipped on the heater and said, "It's been a long day."

She turned one of the vents toward her. "I'm always cold. Poor circulation. Someday, when I get enough money together, I'm going to move to L.A. That's where the music is, anyway. L.A.!" She trilled it, as if it were the top note on the scale. "Then I'll never be cold again."

I shifted into first and started down St. Gregory toward the Parkway. I wasn't really sure where I was going, but after Sophie and Irene Croft, and pal Joey, I wanted off the Hill as quickly as I could go.

I headed southwest when I got to Columbia, along the riverfront. At that time of the morning, the streets were deserted and the city looming behind them looked as sedate and unpeopled as midnight in the suburbs. I got off the Parkway at Vine and drove through the greenish haze of street lights to Central. Nothing was moving on the sidewalks but bits of paper, chased by the wind.

Nothing was lit up but the traffic lights and the arc lamps overhead. The great marble and glass skyscrapers towered up on either side of us, with no one but caretakers and janitors inside. Some cities never sleep—you can never really have them all to yourself. Cincinnati sleeps each night like it's drugged. And coasting through it at three in the morning you can still get that small-town sense of scale, that reassuring feeling that, in spite of the marble and the brass, this is one city that's not bigger than you are.

When we got to Central Parkway, I turned west, skirting the half of the city above Twelfth. I still didn't know where I was going. In a way, I suppose, I was waiting for Grace to tell me. But she just huddled in front of the heater, rubbing her hands together and humming little scat-like tunes. I figured she was content to end up wherever I took her. Which gave me the sinking feeling that she'd made this kind of trip before. Say every night at closing time. To every point on the compass. With whoever was left in the bar. I was as vain as the next man, but I certainly didn't credit myself with attracting a girl as young and as offbeat as this one was—a girl who seemed to be habitually bopping along to the soulful sound of some old Philco, tuned to a station that only she could hear. Besides, I didn't feel any heat coming off her. She'd been friendly, and in her own goofy way, kind of disarming; but she seemed as cold inside as she was on the outside. Which only made me more certain that what we had in common was the contents of my wallet. If she was a whore, she had a hell of an act. If she was just an oddball looking for company and a few extra dollars—which seemed more likely—she was still a strange fish.

123

When we hit the Fairmount hillside, she helped bring the question into focus by skipping a beat in her songs and saying, "You live around here?"

"Pretty close."

She went back to her humming, and I decided to say it outright.

"You want to come home with me?"

She looked up as if she'd heard the schoolbell ring. "Of course. That was the idea, wasn't it?" She gave me a searching look and I started to feel very old.

"What's your problem?" she said.

I glanced over at her and asked, "What's my name?"

"You're the detective who likes Billie Holiday," she replied, as if that were a sufficient answer. "Don't be a goof. I like the way you look. I like this raggedy old car. And I'm going to like what happens when we go to bed."

"You always do what you like?"

She stared at me as if the question made no sense. "Shit, yes. Don't you?"

I didn't answer her. She kept looking at me and I kept looking at the road. She finally said, "What *is* your problem? Is it my age? I'm twenty-two. Or I will be in July. Want to see my driver's license?"

I shook my head.

"Then what is it?" She didn't give me a chance to reply. "I'll tell you what your problem is. You think too much with this"—she tapped her head—"and not enough with this." She put her hand on her groin. "I know. I used to be just like you. When I came to school here three years ago, I was all head. I went to classes and did my homework, and when a boy put his hands on my tits, I pretended I didn't like it. I pretended I was learning about music, too, by reading books and listening

124

to lectures. But jazz isn't learned in a classroom. And life isn't either. It's got to be lived on its own terms. And you can't do that by pretending."

She sounded twenty-one, all right. I didn't bother to point out that you can't discover what life's terms are by doing everything that you want to do, either. It would have been too easy to say, and, besides, as clichéd as it was, there was a good deal of truth in what Grace had said. It wasn't a very complicated truth, and you had to be young to feel it fully. Young and enthusiastic. Listening to her made me feel a little adolescent fire in my own veins. And it also reminded me of just how powerful and attractive the feeling of freedom can be, when you are twenty-one. Or fourteen, like Robbie Segal.

"Well," she said to me. "Are we going to your place? Or are we going to pretend that you're too old to want to fuck me? And that I'm too young to want to be fucked?"

When she put it that way, I couldn't see where I had much of a choice.

Afterward, I could see it. And feel it, too. Guilt, thick as ether, seeped into my body, leaving me with a numbed, heavy heart. Grace would have said, "If you couldn't handle it, you shouldn't have done it." And she would have been absolutely right. I sat beside her in bed, smoking a cigarette and thinking miserably of how far I had traveled from the days when doing what you wanted to do had seemed the essence of life.

I fell asleep, holding that melancholy thought to my breast, and woke up—a good eight hours later—to the taste of Grace's mouth on my lips.

From the way my body responded to that kiss, I

125

thought, "You could have been wrong last night." The phone saved me from sin by ringing suddenly and stridently on the bedstand.

"Let it go," whispered Grace.

But I pulled away and sat up—like a soldier at reveille. Glanced at the clock, which was showing eleven-thirty, and knew at once who it was. With Grace nibbling my shoulder, I sloughed off the last of the night and picked up the receiver.

"Harry?"

"Yes, Mildred," I said. "It's me."

"I've been worried," she said a little frantically. "I tried getting you at the office, but there wasn't any answer."

I pried one of Grace's spidery arms from my chest and said, "I overslept. I had a late night."

Grace fell back on the bed with a laugh. Mildred must have overheard her, because I could hear her stiffening up on the other end of the line—a sound like a rubber raft being inflated. "I see," she said.

"Mildred," I said in my soberest voice, "I was looking for Robbie last night. And I may have gotten a lead."

"Yes?" she said and her voice became warm and eager. "She's all right?"

Grace said, "Who's Robbie?" And I tossed a hand at her to shut up.

"Harry?" Mildred said again. "*Is* she all right?"

She was trying. I could hear it in her voice—a sliver of patience, put there like a tab in a shirt collar to give it shape and steadiness. I wanted desperately to give her something in return. But the best I could do was say, "I think so. I'll find out more this afternoon."

She didn't say anything. I think she was afraid to speak.

Afraid all her fears would come tumbling out uncontrollably, as they had on the previous day.

"You're doing well," I said to fill the silence. "You're doing better than anyone could expect, Mildred. But you've got to hold on a bit longer."

"I don't know—"

I didn't let her finish. "You're a tough lady and you can do it."

"Perhaps," she admitted. "Madge Rostow came to visit me yesterday, did you know that?"

"I knew."

"I didn't think I could talk about this with anyone but you," Mildred said with a curious detachment. "I just didn't think I could do it."

"Did talking to her help?" I asked her.

"I don't know. Yes, I think it did. Today I don't feel quite as alone."

"That's good."

"Perhaps," she said again. "I don't like telling other people my problems. It seems so . . . cowardly."

I knew what she meant. I hadn't been raised on a street like Eastlawn Drive for nothing. I'd absorbed some of that fierce sense of propriety, too. And I hadn't rebelled against that propriety without picking up some of Grace's larkish brand of selfishness. As I sat there with the girl lying beside me and Mildred searching for words on the phone, they seemed to me to be two halves of the same mysterious whole.

I said something about her being more courageous than cowardly. But that was beside the point.

"I don't know why," she said, "but I feel as if I've violated a trust. Do you know what I mean?"

I said, "You've stopped pretending everything was all

right. And on a street like yours, that's a hard thing to do."

"I feel like I've let them down. I could almost see it in Madge's eyes. She was sweet and supportive, but she was frightened, too. I actually ended up telling her everything was going to be all right." She laughed delicately. "I think that's what made me feel better."

It was a strange way to find hope—to curtsey your way into it, like greeting royalty. But in that mandarin world of hers, perhaps it was the *only* way of finding it. Politeness, the show of neighborliness, were as much the cornerstones of Eastlawn Drive philosophy as the unreal, prideful show of prosperity. And if it took seeing Madge Rostow losing her cool for Mildred to feel obliged to recover her own stamina, that was all right, too.

"I'll call you when I have some news, Mildred," I said. "You'll be fine until then."

"Yes," she said without conviction, "I'll be all right."

I hung up the phone and turned to my other problem, who was lying naked beside me. She was so skinny her ribs showed through the flesh like a child's green bones.

"Don't you ever eat, Grace?" I said.

She rubbed her flat tummy. "I'm dieting."

I laughed out loud. "For God's sake, why?"

She turned on her elbow and one small breast fell against the pillow. "I don't like to put anything into my body that isn't natural."

"What about me?"

She grinned. "That's high-grade protein. Anyway, if I had to give that up, I'd find a different diet."

I gazed at her with amusement.

"I thought we'd spend the day in bed," she said lazily.

"I've got to go to work."

128

"Won't it wait?"

I glanced at her again and said, "I'm afraid not."

She sat up as if she'd been shot from a cannon. "O.K.," she said. "I get the message. Time for Grace to go."

Life on its own terms apparently didn't preclude childish displays of temper when those terms weren't to your liking. I mentioned this to her and she snarled at me.

"Well, what's so goddamn important, anyway?"

"A girl named Robbie Segal."

"Is she the bitch in that photograph in your coat pocket?"

I gave her a look and she stared right back at me.

"I went through your coat last night," she said with brazen nonchalance. "I took some money, too."

I shook my head.

"Nothing's for free, Harry," she said with a shrug. "And I've got to live."

"Then you owe me something," I said, pointing a finger at her.

"I owe you dick," she said. "However, I like you. So I'll do you a favor." She pulled the sheet up to her hips and said, "That girl in the picture . . . I've seen her before. She was with some kid—a guitarist for The Furies—in The Pentangle on Sunday night. She seemed to be having a *real* good time," she added a little nastily.

"What do you mean by that?"

"I mean she was drunk on her ass and hitting on anything wearing pants. It was almost funny, seeing how young and cherry she was. Real pretty but not too cool. The kid she was with practically had to sock her to get her out of the bar."

I described Bobby Caldwell to her and said, "Was he the one?"

She nodded. "He's a good guitarist, too. I felt bad for him. He had to cut the last set short just to keep her from taking her pants off."

I said, "Was Theo Clinger there, too?"

"No," she said.

But she said it too quickly and forcefully, as if she'd been expecting me to ask her about Clinger and had already prepared an answer. She hadn't liked Robbie Segal. I could hear that in her voice. Which would make lying that much easier.

"You like Theo?" I asked her.

"I love him," she said passionlessly. "He's a great musician. And he's been very good to me. He gave me a place to live when I had nowhere else to go. He took care of me and taught me something important about life and music."

"And what was that?"

"That you make it up yourself from what's inside you."

"You wouldn't want to tell me where the guru could be found, would you?"

Grace stared at me for a moment, then wormed away across the bed and reached down and picked up her skimpy bra and panties. Silently she began to dress. I watched her for a second and felt a little bad that we were ending like this—like two strangers in a hotel room with folding money on the dresser. And then thought that this was probably the only way it could have ended with Grace. Her face told me that. She was so used to this scene that she didn't even look disappointed. Just a little restless and abstracted, like a workman packing up his tools at the end of a bad day.

16

IT WAS ALMOST TWELVE-THIRTY WHEN I DROPPED
Grace off on the sunny Mt. Adams sidewalk. We hadn't
said much to each other as I drove. She'd quickly lost
herself in that private world of hers—humming a bar of
jazz, improvising a snatch of lyrics, drumming her
fingers on the black straw purse. And I had been too busy
thinking about Robbie Segal to pay this other lost girl
much attention. It wasn't until I actually dropped her off
on Monastery and watched her walking away in her
feathered hat and tight print dress—her skinny legs
wobbling on tall black heels—that I realized that I hadn't
said goodbye to her. I thought about calling her back, but
deep down and in spite of the way she'd helped me, I
knew that I didn't really want to be involved any further
with Grace. So I let her go without a word. Watched her
drift up Monastery to St. Gregory's—skimming her hand
across the glistening metal tops of the parking meters—
and when I lost her in the heavy, black shadows of the
monastery, I slipped the Pinto back into gear and drove
down the hill to town.

As soon as I got to the office, I cleaned the litter of

circulars and bills off my desk, took a yellow pad and pencil out of the drawer, and began to write down a brief outline of what I knew about Robbie Segal's disappearance.

Sunday, early afternoon: Mildred and Robbie argue over money Robbie has taken from her purse. Mildred leaves. Returns at 4:30 to find Robbie gone.

Sunday, late afternoon: Pastor Caldwell sees his son and Robbie in the back yard of the apartment house.

Sunday evening. Bobby and Robbie are seen at The Pentangle Club.

I put the pencil down.

I only had one day partially filled in, with Monday and Tuesday still complete blanks. But that was a good deal more than I'd had the day before. Plus, I was now certain that Bobby Caldwell had helped my runaway escape from Eastlawn Drive. Judging from the photograph of her and Clinger, and from the Pentangle T-shirt and the other drug- and sex-related paraphernalia that Bobby had given her, I figured that the Caldwell boy had spent the past few months priming Robbie to run away—convincing her to "come out and play," as he'd asked her to do in the love song. Only young Robbie had apparently taken what Bobby Caldwell had said to heart. On Sunday night, she'd begun to play in earnest. And Bobby hadn't liked it one bit.

If I could read him correctly—and I had the feeling that I could, after all I'd learned—Bobby had never

132

intended that his girl should take an active part in the Pentangle scene. I guessed that he'd taken her with him to the club on Sunday night because he hadn't wanted to leave her alone on her first night away from home and because the music he made at the bar was an important facet of his life. Maybe the most important facet. Because he was made of music, this kid. All of his friends had said so. Irene, Grace, even Clinger (by report) had said so, too. Music and Robbie Segal were all he'd thought about. I could only imagine how disappointed he must have felt when he'd discovered on Sunday evening that Robbie was no longer listening to what he played.

I'd sensed it all along—that this beautiful girl-child had wanted something more than Bobby could offer her. And while the ugly scene at the bar could have been a fluke—a combination of too much beer and too much excitement—it could also have been a sign of things to come, a first declaration of independence from her mother and from Bobby, as well. Maybe it had been Clinger and The Pentangle Club that she'd been looking for all along—a world in which she could make up her own rules as she went along. Or maybe she hadn't known what she'd wanted, except to taste life, as Grace had been trying to do, on its own terms. Whatever it had been, she was getting beyond her lover by Sunday night, launching herself on her own erratic course, with Bobby trailing somewhere behind her, holding on for dear life.

Whether the boy had been able to catch up before Wednesday, or whether Robbie had gone off entirely on her own, I didn't know. For her sake, I hoped she'd broken free. Because if she hadn't, she was surely implicated in what had happened to her lover. What had happened to him might very well have happened to her, too.

I pushed the yellow pad away from me, as if I were pushing the thought out of my mind. But the bad feeling had already started up—the dread. Two and a half days were scarcely enough time for Robbie to lose the Caldwell boy entirely. Even if she'd wanted to lose him, *he* wouldn't have let go that quickly. And in spite of the way I'd been speculating about her, there was no indication that she hadn't felt an affection for the boy who'd helped her run away. In fact, she might have loved him as deeply as he'd loved her and still have wanted something more—some forbidden excitement, some deep, improbable sin, to wipe out all those years of decency and of Mildred. And if she'd loved him at all, she wouldn't have ditched him the day after she'd left home. That would have been too cold, too calculating. And the girl I'd been looking for—learning about and partly creating—wasn't capable of that kind of callousness.

I stared at the pad again—at that last entry. And wrote down one name: *Clinger?* I needed more information on him, and I knew where I might be able to find a bit of it. I picked up the phone and dialed Dino Taylor, a disc jockey at WGUC. I got through to his secretary, who told me that Dino wouldn't be free until three o'clock. That left me two hours to kill. And as I hung up the phone, I knew I wasn't going to be able to spend them sitting in the office, staring at the bare, yellow walls. Not in the mood I'd worked myself into.

So I got up and walked out the door. Took the elevator down to the lobby and stepped into the daylight. I didn't really have a destination in mind as I headed up Vine Street, but once I got to the Square, I found myself walking north, amid the car sounds and the slick, made-up faces and the white blanketing light of the afternoon sun, toward the Enquirer Building on Sixth. I had a few contacts on the paper—one man in particular who wrote a weekly pop music column. I figured there was a decent chance he could tell me something useful about Clinger.

I pushed on against the flow of afternoon shoppers, stopping once at the dark, diamond-shaped windows of The Cricket restaurant, where the sweet, oily smell of grilled meat and the brothy aroma of dark German beer held me for a moment. I managed to pull myself away and walk twenty feet farther up the sidewalk to the bronze revolving doors of the newspaper office. Inside the lobby the elevator captain showed me to a car of my own. And a moment later I stepped out into a paneled corridor with the paper's logo fashioned in metal on the wall. A pretty, black-haired receptionist in a camel-colored sweater smiled at me as if I'd been expected.

"Who did you want to see?" she said sweetly.

"Jack Leonard," I told her.

She looked at me as if I'd broken her heart. "I'm afraid he's out of town on assignment. Is there anyone else who could help you?"

Outside of a few hooligans on the sports desk, the only other staffer I knew well enough to mention was Marcie Shaeffer of the society, gossip, and weddings page. And I wasn't so sure I wanted to talk to Marcie. I'd actually done a job for her several years before, and it had left a very bad taste. At the time she'd been divorcing her husband, an architect named Leo Shaeffer. Her lawyers had hired me to look after her until the legal proceedings were completed. I'd thought I'd been hired for protection—that was certainly the impression that Marcie

135

gave me. In fact, I'd worked up quite a grudge against
Leo by the time we met in court. But he turned out to
be a gentle, neurotic young man with the caved-in, dark-
eyed, peccant look of failure already written on his face.
He sat on the bench, head bent, vacant-eyed, listening
to the lawyers as if, in his mind, he was as guilty as Marcie
had claimed he was. By the time the hearing was over,
I'd begun to think that the only thing the poor son-of-a-
bitch was truly guilty of was loving his wife.

Marcie Shaeffer was a rich, pretty, spoiled girl who'd
been raised to believe that she had a gift for anything
she put her hand to, as if talent were one of her guar-
anteed rights. But like most talentless people, her only
real gift was for self-indulgence. She dabbled in everything from water colors to modern dance, saw a shrink
four times a week, and came home to torment Leo for
standing in the way of her fulfillment. The sad part was
that the poor son-of-a-bitch believed her. He'd spent six
years tripping over himself, trying to get out of Marcie's way. And one afternoon, when he hadn't moved
fast enough, she'd attempted suicide and nearly broken
him in two. She filed for divorce the next day, which
was the best thing that could have happened to Leo,
although he didn't know it. I wondered, at the time,
if he ever would. She'd gone on to a career as a gossip
columnist, where she could spread the blame for her
failures more evenly among her friends. As for Leo, I
didn't know what had become of him, although as I
stood there in front of the pretty receptionist, trying to
make up my mind about whether or not to ask for Ms.
Shaeffer, I wondered if he'd finally found the strength
to forgive himself.

Thinking about Leo certainly didn't make me feel like

talking to Marcie. She wasn't likely to know anything about Theo Clinger, anyway. He didn't run with her crowd, although it occurred to me that Irene Croft probably did.

Not that I considered the Croft woman a likely suspect in Robbie's disappearance. She seemed like too big a leap for a teenage runaway from Eastlawn Drive to make in her first days away from home. But Irene was linked with Clinger. Judging from the throb in her voice when she'd mentioned his name and the look of rapture in her eyes in that photograph, she was one of his most devoted followers. And if worse came to worst, I might need someone like the Croft woman to lead me to the Lost Prince—someone I could pressure into cooperating with me.

I sighed aloud and told the receptionist, "Marcie Shaeffer, then. Tell her Harry Stoner."

The girl jabbed a button on her intercom, whispered my name into a speaker, and looked up at me with a satisfied smile. A moment later, Marcie came strolling down the hall.

She had gained a few pounds since I'd last seen her. They added fullness to her hips and a bit of sag to her fleshy jaw. But aside from that, she looked like the same, bitchy, self-involved young woman I'd known three years before. Rusty blonde hair, swept back in a bouffant that hugged her round face like a tiara. Wax-red lips. Pale gray eyes shaped like tear drops. Cleft chin. Heavily powdered and dressed to the nines, she looked like Cincinnati's idea of royalty, although the idea was entirely her own. She wore a gold charm bracelet on her right wrist. It tinkled like crystal when she raised a cigarette to her lips.

"Harry?" she said in a voice as dark and sticky as damson jelly. "What can I do for you?"

"I'd like to talk to you for a moment."

"Why not?" She jerked the cigarette from her mouth, scattering ashes on the receptionist, whirled on her high heels, and sauntered back down the hall. I glanced at the receptionist before trailing after Marcie. She was staring at her desk as if she was searching it for a weapon.

Marcie led me through a glass door to her cubicle in the editorial section. The big white room was lit by fluorescent panels and filled with metal desks and shirt-sleeved reporters and the faint hum of computerized typewriters. Sitting there in that black wool skirt and gold bodice, Marcie looked like a showroom manikin that had been dropped off at the wrong address.

"So what can I do for you, Harry?" she said in a tone that was meant to suggest that I was already getting in her way—like poor, hapless Leo—keeping her from important, fulfilling work. Three years of independence hadn't changed her much and it depressed me.

I pretended she was human and said, "What can you tell me about Irene Croft?"

Marcie arched an eyebrow and made a little, noiseless "o" with her lips. "Is she a client of yours?"

I shook my head.

"You aren't fucking her, are you?" she said with malicious delight.

I shook my head again, but she smiled knowingly.

"I could see it. She's supposed to be a pretty good piece of tail. Or thigh. Or whip, maybe?" Her laugh was like the sound of her bracelet. "What did you do? Pick her up in a bar down on Fourth Street? Did she take you up to the penthouse and show you the sights?"

138

I let her have her laugh, then said, "It's quite a view."

Marcie's mouth dropped open in a cloud of cigarette smoke. "You're kidding," she said. "You really did go up there with her?" She wagged her finger at me. "Better watch out. She's too rich for your blood, Harry, old boy. I'd advise you to stick to your cocktail waitresses and go-go girls. This one is a Croft. And you know what that means."

"Old money," I said.

"Old money and clout," she said with an explosive "t" at the end of clout. "They could knock you right out of this life, if they wanted to. Better steer clear of her, Harry. You're stepping way up in class."

"You think she's classy, Marcie?" I said drily.

She smirked at me and said, "I think she's nuts. Totally bonkers. But she's also a Croft, even if her family would prefer to think otherwise. They've been trying to sweep her under the rug for years. But she just won't stay swept. They've tried to commit her. They've tried to probate her. They've tried shipping her out of the state. But she's outsmarted them every time. She's like a very bad penny. The Crofts can't get rid of her, so they pretend to ignore her. At least, they do until someone like you comes snooping along. Then all bets are off. The Crofts are a very neat family, Harry. There's been a lot of money spent, a lot of strings pulled to keep Irene on the sweet side of notoriety. They're the kind of rich for whom cover-ups were invented. Old English stock. Fifteen generations of Puritan blood. Cofounders of Ivorydale and the squeaky clean ethics of this town. They're the closest thing to aristocracy we've got. They're the Olympians. And all they do is sit up on that hill of theirs in Mt. Lookout and spruce the family tree. Irene was inevitable. If she hadn't come along, they'd have had to invent her."

"Why couldn't they just cut her off without a cent?" I said to Marcie.

"She's got her own trust. Iron-clad millions. And, to be honest, she's fairly shrewd about money. After all, she *is* a Croft. What she spends, she spends wisely. On art and on budding artists."

"Which artists?"

"Oh, she's gone through quite a few. Some of them are famous now. She sets them up. Promotes them. And when she gets bored, she moves on to someone new. But she never forgets to get her money's worth—in paintings and in guarantees of future work. Like I said, she's a shrewd lady."

"Who's her protegé at the moment?" I asked.

Marcie shrugged. "I don't know. Could be anybody. Sometimes Irene bankrolls a loser, simply because he is as strange as she is. I think it's her way of making friends." Marcie eyed me shrewdly. "She's got some pretty kinky tastes, Harry. The kind you've got to pay to indulge."

"You mean kinky sex?" I said, thinking of Rudy and Sophie.

"Drugs, too, from what I hear."

"Does the name Theo Clinger ring any bells?"

"No," she said. "But it's a full-time job keeping up with Irene. Is he her newest find?"

I said, "He might be."

Marcie stubbed out her cigarette in an ashtray, brushing the butt back and forth against the glass as if she was dabbing paint on a canvas. "I might be able to use that," she mused. She dropped the butt delicately into the tray and asked, "What does he do?"

140

"He plays the guitar," I said. "Jazz."

"That's a new one. Where can I find him?"

"I don't know," I said. "Why don't you ask Irene? And if you find out, give me a call."

"I might," she said lazily.

I got up from the chair and said, "Thanks."

Marcie leaned back and gave me a frank look. "You still haven't forgiven me for Leo, have you, Harry?"

"There was nothing to forgive," I said. "What happened was between you and him."

"No," she said with a wistful laugh. "I think this argument is between you and the world." She leaned forward again and smiled affectionately. "You're like a kid, Harry. That's your charm. You're still living in a place where good and bad are something more than scary little words from the past. I've never really understood that."

"I know," I said.

Her eyes veiled and she stared at the ashtray on her desk. "You're all alone, Harry. Just like the rest of us. And no one cares." She dipped a forefinger in the ashes and stirred them listlessly. "No one cares, so why should you?"

I started to tell her, but she held up a hand and waved goodbye with her fingertips. "I don't really want to know," she said.

17

ON MY WAY BACK DOWN VINE I STOPPED AT THE Cricket's front window again, and this time went inside, into the dark tap room, and treated myself to some of that beef and dark German beer. I felt as if I'd earned a break after talking to Marcie Shaeffer, whose bitchiness seemed untempered by the years. Still, I'd felt a bit sorry for Marcie that afternoon. Perhaps because she seemed worried that I disapproved of her. Perhaps because I did disapprove. I sat in one of The Cricket's dark wood booths, eating noodles and roast beef and thinking of Marcie and of Irene Croft—two spoiled women without a talent for anything but the easy art of self-indulgence. They just got their kicks in different ways—Marcie by bitching and tattling and Irene by indulging in gilded depravities. But then I didn't really have the right to point a finger at either one because I could use what Marcie had told me, and I was beginning to think I could use Irene, as well.

If the Croft woman did, in fact, have a patron-client relationship with Theo Clinger, it would go a long way toward explaining the look on her face in the photograph and the throb in her voice when she'd mentioned his name. If he was her newest "discovery," it might have given her a reason to steer me away from him. Which wasn't to say that she'd been lying to me when she'd said that Robbie Segal had been nowhere near Clinger earlier in the week. Just that she could have had a reason to lie—an investment to protect.

I stared out the diamond-shaped windows at the snowy glare of sunlight reflecting off chrome bumpers and shop doors, and decided to pay Irene Croft another visit, after I'd talked with Dino Taylor. I swallowed the last of the beer, which had begun to taste like sweet beef tea, paid my chit at the cash register, and walked back out into the day. I ambled through the sunshine to the Parkade. Picked up the Pinto and headed north again— to Clifton and WGUC.

It was almost three when I got to Central Parkway, and a quarter past by the time I pulled into the cool, multilevel concrete garage of the College Conservatory of Music. WGUC was the University of Cincinnati's radio station. Unlike most college stations, it was a very classy operation, run by professionals for the most part rather than by students, and geared exclusively to the NPR crowd. It seemed an odd place for an old-fashioned D.J. like Dino Taylor to be working. But in spite of his top-40's voice and sleek good looks, Dino was almost an academic when it came to the music he loved. His daily jazz show was as classy as the rest of the GUC operation—a pleasant combination of old standbys and new wave, spiced with the affectionate patter and personal anecdotes of a man who'd spent his whole life among musicians.

I'd first met him at a reception I'd been hired to

143

chaperon. But I hadn't ended up doing much chaperoning that night, mainly because the rock group for whom the reception was being given didn't show up until the wee hours of the morning and by then the boys were too drunk and fagged out to cause any mischief. I spent most of the evening talking with Dino, or listening to him talk about the music he loved. We'd bumped into one another a couple of times since then, and, although I didn't consider him a friend, I thought I knew him well enough to ask him about Theo Clinger.

I took the elevator from the garage to the ground floor, followed a series of arrows through wandering corridors full of pretty girls in tights and toe shoes and thin, bearded, serious-looking young men carrying buckram instrument cases, and eventually wound up at the GUC complex in the north end of the building.

A secretary sitting at a desk inside the plate glass door directed me to an empty office. And a few minutes after I'd sat down, Dino stepped into the room.

"Only got a minute, Harry," he said in his smooth announcer's baritone. "Have to go to some goddamn meeting at the Convention Center."

He seated himself behind the desk and gave me a grin that was as smooth and pally as his voice. He was a bit of a con man, Dino. But then most D.J.s were. In a business where you have to make your voice smile and caper for three to four hours every day, it's hard not to develop the thin, theatrical mannerisms of an actor. The fulsome warmth and instant rapport grated on me a little, after the time I'd spent with Marcie Shaeffer. So did Dino's razor-cut good looks, which struck me that afternoon as being too controlled and too varnished, like a brand new toupee. They were the perfect match for his facile voice and easy air of intimacy; and for that very reason seemed vaguely phoney, like Marcie Shaeffer's brand of sophistication.

"C'mon, Harry," he rasped. "Time's awastin'."

"What can you tell me about Theo Clinger," I said to him.

He folded his hands behind his immaculate gray hair and smiled benignly. "Ah, Theo. Hell of a musician. He could have been something else, ten years ago. That is, if he hadn't gotten stuck in this jerkwater town."

"What kept him here?"

"He didn't have the guts to leave, for one thing. Tremendous talent, no ambition. It's an old story. And for another, why be a little fish in a big pond when you can have the little pond all to yourself. Theo's owned the avant-garde jazz scene in this city for the last decade. He is new wave in Cincinnati. The king. He's got devout followers all over the Midwest."

"I've heard about them," I said. "He likes them kind of young, doesn't he?"

Dino grinned. "Sure, he has his groupies. Every musician has. But he treats them a helluva lot better than most musicians do." Dino unlocked his hands from behind his head and leaned toward me with the air of a car salesman closing a deal. "I don't know why you're asking me about him. I don't think I want to know. But understand, Harry, I like this man. To me, Theo Clinger is the sixties incarnate. Free love, communal living, dope, spiritual raps, a willingness to experiment. He's got it all. He treats his groupies like a family. They share in everything—work and play. And they live the kind of life that most of us only dreamed about when we were twenty. Hey, I'm not saying it's for everyone. But it's one way to go."

"Opting out?" I said.

Dino shook his head. "Theo's no dropout. He lives the sixties dream, all right. But the sixties had its pragmatic side, too. Let me tell you a story: the other day I was shopping lower Clifton and I came across a new shop on Ludlow—a fancy boutique specializing in imported jewelry. Real nice set-up. I walked in and looked at the guy behind the counter and did a double take. He's got long hair, wears wire rims, muttonchops. Like John Sebastian at Woodstock, you know? I said to him, 'Didn't you used to make beaded belts up in Clifton in the days of peace and love?' And he just smiled. It was the same guy, Harry.

"Old hippies aren't drop-outs, they're drop-ins. Theo's no different. He plays at Eden. But he sells tickets at the gate. His talent was great at one time. He was a real innovator, in the Cage mold. But the days of Cage are dead and gone. And Theo's no youngster any more. He hasn't got what he once had, and he knows it. In fact, he planned for it, like a Yankee farmer. Back in his salad days, he bought up properties all over Mt. Adams and Clifton. Bookstores, small shops, clubs. Over the years, he's rehabbed most of them. He used to be one of the bigger property owners in the city. They weren't prime lots, but they turned a profit. Or at least they did up until a few years ago. I heard he's been having some problems lately. I guess inflation and tight money hit him as hard as it hit everyone else. I know for a fact that he had to sell his bookstore and restaurant. But he'll fix things up. He's a good businessman. To be honest, that's one of the reasons he takes such good care of his family—it's a cheap source of labor."

"You're telling me he's an entrepreneur?" I said with a laugh.

146

"Damn right. Theo'll do just about anything for a buck. Hell, when you have an empire to protect, you've got to be shrewd. And Theo likes being emperor."

"Does he have a central office?" I said. "One place that he lives in or works out of?"

"He used to have a place in Mt. Adams," Dino said. "But I hear he's moved to the country. To Kentucky, I think. Don't ask me where."

"You *do* like him, don't you, Dino?"

He leaned back in the chair and stared dreamily at the wall behind me. "Sure, I like him. Who wouldn't like the life he leads? He makes music and he lives in paradise. Who wouldn't like that?"

Free love, music, the communion of like-minded souls. It not only sounded like the sixties, it sounded like an adolescent's dream of freedom. It hurt me a little to think that, all along, the two might have been one. But it made me that much surer that Clinger's family was where Robbie Segal had been headed from the start. A world that seemed to be the moral and emotional opposite of Eastlawn Drive. And yet, if what Dino said were true, the two worlds weren't as far apart as they appeared to be. Even paradise had to be paid for in cash. And trailing behind money-making, like its very own shadow, were all the doubts and uncertainties, all the fears and debts that made Eastlawn Drive such a nervous, conformable street. Every lifestyle has its price tag, and the cost is always figured in the same compromises. If the responsibilities of kingship had turned Clinger into a capitalist, he'd bought some capitalist values, too. Otherwise, there would be no way for him to turn a profit. The more of those values Clinger had bought, the closer to Eastlawn Drive paradise must have come. And hard times had probably brought them even closer together.

I wondered whether it would break Robbie's spirit to discover that she wasn't a high-flying angel, she was cheap labor. I also wondered why an entrepreneur like Clinger would need a patroness like Irene Croft behind him. Perhaps it flattered his vanity to think that a very rich, very influential lady thought he was God. It was a reasonable assumption. Only Dino had emphasized that Clinger was a shrewd businessman, too. And Irene Croft was apparently no philanthropist. If he'd taken up with a woman who was going to end up costing him something, I figured he'd done it for a good reason. Maybe some trouble in paradise that had to be paid for in hard cash. The possibility made talking to Irene Croft seem an even better idea than it had before.

While I was thinking it over, Dino got up and walked to the door. "Gotta go, Harry," he said cheerfully.

"One last question?" I said.

He leaned against the door. "All right."

"Have you heard of a group called The Furies?"

He pinched the bridge of his nose between his thumb and forefinger. "Yeah, I think I might have heard of them," he said. "Local rock group? Good lead guitarist?"

"That's the one," I said. "Do you know where I could find them?"

"They play Mt. Adams a lot, I think. Try Corky's Bar on Hill Street." He ducked out the door, then stuck his head back into the room. "But don't try the food," he said.

18

IT WAS FOUR-THIRTY BY THE TIME I GOT TO THE HIGH-land House on Celestial Street. The late afternoon sun had already dropped down in the western sky, casting a golden wash of light on the Ohio and burnishing the great, forested ridges of the Kentucky shore. Everything on top of Mt. Adams was bathed in a warm, yellow glow. Sunlight hung in the frosted porcelain globes of the street lamps, burned like candles in each window of the tall, reddish high-rises, and winked from every porch railing and fixture. It was even netted in the green, crooked mulberries and maple trees, turning their trunks to pillars of gold. The day seemed to have caught fire. I stood by the Pinto in the Celestial lot, watching it burn.

And for a moment, I felt the time of year as strongly as I had when I was a kid—when it had filled me with a leering, mysterious joy. I had to make myself shake the feeling off before I crossed the deserted street to the red-canopied entryway of the apartment house. And being forced to slough it off made me aware of the absurdity of my profession—of a job that was forever out of season, buried always, like some rusted spade, beneath deep, December snow.

By the time I'd gotten to the lobby—past the doorman with his smiling, rubber face and into the ornate, candle-lit stillness of the restaurant anteroom, where the only sounds were the barks of chairs being set up for the evening and the plate noises of table-setting being arranged—I'd sobered up. It may not have been a season for detectives, but it wasn't the hour for childishness, either. I forced myself back into the job, like a man donning a uniform. Walked over to the house phone and dailed 2201.

I let it ring several times, rehearsing in my mind what I would say if she answered. What I wanted from Irene Croft was a detailed description of how Clinger and his family lived. What I wanted was a map that would lead me straight to Robbie Segal. Because Dino Taylor had only given me the rough outline of Clinger's setup, and even that had been colored by his affectionate regard for the Lost Prince and his brave new world. Under differ-ent circumstances, I would have found something to ad-mire there, too, since I was as much a child of the sixties as Dino or Clinger was. I wanted to believe that Clinger's Eden was, indeed, a realm of peace and love. I wanted to believe that Robbie Segal was sitting there at that moment, having a good time. Only I couldn't con myself into thinking that an entrepreneur like Theo Clinger was a saintly Mr. Natural. Or that kinky Irene Croft fit into anybody's version of Eden.

The phone kept buzzing, and I kept spinning out sce-narios. On the tenth ring, somebody picked up the line.

"Who is it?" Irene Croft said in her mellow, familiar voice.

"It's Harry Stoner, Ms. Croft. I want to talk to you for a minute."

"What about?" she said.

"About Theo Clinger and Robbie Segal."

"But I already told you what I knew about them. Or do you want to hear it, again? Theo knows nothing about the girl. Got that? He is a good and kind man—a lot better than the world realizes." She said the last part with a curious bitterness.

I had the feeling that she was carrying on an argument that she'd been having with someone else. There was a ripe note of fury in her voice. "That may be," I said. "But I want to know where to find him."

"I told you—The Pentangle Club."

"I mean the place where he lives, Irene. With that family of his."

She didn't say anything for a moment. "I already told you that Robbie wasn't there," she said coolly. "Or do you think I was lying?"

"I think I'd like to see for myself."

"Well, I don't think I'm going to tell you, Mr. Stoner. I don't think I care to see Theo tormented by you."

"Don't make me go to the police and the newspapers, Irene," I said.

She laughed bitterly, as if she was tickled to discover that I was just as rotten as the rest of the world—all those philistines who didn't have the taste to appreciate Theo's genius. "You'd do that?"

"I wouldn't like to. But I want to talk to Clinger."

"You're playing with fire, Stoner," she said with that same bitter amusement. "And you're going to discover that I'm a hard lady to blackmail."

I thought of what Marcie had told me and said, "That's

151

probably true. But Theo doesn't have your connections, Irene. What do you think the cops would say about his stable of underaged playmates?"

"I take your point," she said after a moment. "But unfortunately you've caught me at a bad time. I simply can't talk right now."

"Make time," I said.

She put her hand over the receiver, then came back on the line. "I'll be down in a couple of minutes," she said and hung up.

I sat down on the same plush chair I'd sat on the night before. I didn't really think I'd shaken the woman up. She was too dry and too cold a character to be shaken by much of anything. Besides, with all the Croft money and power behind her she had little to fear, personally, from newspaper reporters or cops. I didn't really understand why she'd decided to talk to me, unless she wanted to find out exactly what kind of monster I was or unless she was genuinely worried about Clinger, who didn't have her money or power to protect him. She didn't seem the type to show loyalty, even to one of her protegés. But if she was trying to protect her boy, the trick would be to keep her worried—to convince her that I was a dangerous article, without revealing that I had next to nothing in the way of hard evidence that would connect Clinger to Robbie. And if I knew Irene, that wasn't going to be an easy trick. She had an ear for lies and for self-deceptions—it was her brand of perfect pitch. But telling her I was going to go to the police wouldn't actually be a lie —I'd already been to them and intended to check in with Bannock before the day was out. And there was no question in my mind that Clinger couldn't stand up to a full-scale police investigation. His very way of life was

152

against the law. The fact that I didn't agree with some of those laws made what I was planning to do seem uglier than mere lying, but I didn't see where I had a choice.

A few minutes went by, and then a bell went off like the timer on a range and the elevator doors opened. A chunky, bald man, dressed in a brown leisure suit and white dress shirt, stepped out and gazed around the lobby until he spotted me on the other side of the plate glass door. His shirt was open at the neck and a pelt of gray hair curled out of the collar, with a gold pendant hanging in the matted hair, like a jewel packed in creosote. He was about forty years old and had a pleasant, tanned face, creased with laugh lines around the blue eyes and the small fleshy mouth. His forehead rose in wrinkles up to his shiny bald pate. He would have looked like a good-natured insurance salesman, if it hadn't been for the pendant and the other gold jewelry he was wearing on his hands and wrists. They gave him a bit of the tawdry flash of a lounge lizard. Only he wasn't good looking enough to be a gigolo. I didn't quite know what to make of him, except that he seemed to be interested in me. He smiled through the glass door, then unlocked it and walked over to where I was sitting. I could smell his aftershave the moment he stepped out of the elevator room—a smell like rotting bananas.

"Hi!" he said in a sharp, merry voice. Even his breath smelled sweet, but that was because he was chewing gum—a little hunk of it that he passed from cheek to cheek with the tip of his tongue. The gum made me think of Sylvia Rostow.

"Jerry Lavelle," the man said and held out his hand.

"Harry Stoner," I said, shaking with him.

"Let's go have a drink, Harry," he said, nodding

toward the restaurant door. "We'll put it on Irene's tab."

I got up and followed him into the Celestial's bar—a dark, leathery cavern, lit by candles in tall, red glass holders. It was virtually empty at that time of the day. We sat at the rail, on leather-capped wooden stools, studded with brass nail heads. The bartender—a big, ruddy man with sleek black hair—seemed to know Lavelle. He smiled at him pleasantly.

"What'll it be, Jerry?" he said in a hushed voice.

"Bourbon for me, Hal."

Lavelle glanced my way and I said, "Johnny Walker Red Label. Straight up."

The bartender pointed a finger at us and winked. "You got it."

While Hal was pouring the drinks into heavy, beveled shot glasses, Lavelle turned on the stool and gave me a grin. "Nice bar. Quiet," he said and cracked his gum.

Hearing the cool note of appraisal in his voice, I suddenly realized who he was. You see men like him in Vegas all the time. Sweet-smelling, tanned, dandified muscle. Not bouncers, exactly. But the guys who are in charge of the beefy boys. Jerry Lavelle was a middle-level hood. A pro. And I couldn't figure out what he'd been doing in Irene Croft's apartment.

"I thought Irene was coming down," I said.

"She can't make it," he said with that merry grin.

"Maybe I ought to come back some other time."

He shook his head. "I don't think so, Harry. I think she's going to be tied up for awhile."

"We had some business to talk over."

"Yeah, I know," he said, adjusting himself on the stool. He was packing iron—I was sure of it from the way he moved his shoulders. "That's what I wanted to talk to you about."

"I'm listening," I said.

The bartender laid the drinks down in front of us. Lavelle picked his up and took a tiny sip. "You got to leave Irene alone, Harry," he said, as he put the drink back down. "Stay out of her life. I'm telling you as a friend."

I stared at my "friend" and said, "What's bourbon taste like through bubble gum?"

He smiled lazily. "Chewy," he said.

He took another sip of booze. "You're a tough guy, aren't you, Harry? Yeah, I can see it. You're a big, tough guy." He cracked his gum again and swirled his swizzle stick through the bourbon. "Look, let's not waste each other's time. You want to talk to Irene and she doesn't want to talk to you. It's that simple."

"I'll go to the cops, Lavelle," I said.

He shook his head, no. "You won't do that, Harry. First of all, I wouldn't let you. And second, the Croft family wouldn't like it. And third, it's just not in your best interest. Irene doesn't know a thing about this girl you're looking for. Trust me on this. I'm not saying the lady in the penthouse is innocent. We both know better than that. Irene's got her problems. And right now, she doesn't need any more of them. It'd be too expensive."

"That's tough," I said.

"Hey, let's be honest with each other," he said cheerfully. "This is a crazy lady we're talking about. A meshuginah. She's an embarrassment to her family. And they don't want to see her name in the papers."

"Just who are you working for, Lavelle?" I said.

"Let's say I'm a friend of the family's."

I got off the stool, dug a couple of dollars out of my pocket, and tossed them on the bar.

"I don't want any trouble, Harry," Lavelle said. "All

I'm asking you to do is leave Irene out of it. What you do otherwise is your business. Just think about it. Promise me you'll think about it."

I brushed past him to the door. As I was walking out of the room, I heard him say to Hal, the bartender, "Look at that. He didn't even touch his drink."

19

I WALKED TO THE CAR AND SAT BEHIND THE WHEEL
for a moment, staring at the apartment building. The sun
was setting above the river in a thin orange band, and
lamplights were beginning to shine through the curtained windows of Highland House. Street lights had
begun to pop on, too, up and down the hill, showering
the sidewalks with pale green light. I looked up at the
top floor of the high-rise, at Irene Croft's penthouse, and
knew that I wasn't going to get back up there without a
warrant—not with Jerry Lavelle on guard.

I simply hadn't counted on a man like Jerry Lavelle,
in spite of what Marcie had told me about the Crofts and
their clout. I suppose I'd thought that they were above
that kind of play—too gentlemanly, too law-and-order
decent. After all, they were the Olympians, as Marcie
had said. They were the social and political elite, who
legislated the rules that the rest of us followed.

I knew they were powerful people. Bedrock, anti-
Roosevelt Republicans, who had solid ties with the police
department and with City Hall. In any given year, a
Croft might have been mayor or municipal judge or

congressman from the first district. They'd been getting a lot of publicity since the Reagan election—Sunday pictorials showing Crofts in riding breeches, sipping tall, cool drinks. I simply hadn't pictured those strict, featureless men turning to hired muscle. It seemed too B-movie for the bluebloods, although when I thought about it I realized they were a B-movie crowd—old-fashioned moralists, without shading or subtlety, except when it came to protecting one of their own. Maybe they'd thought that Lavelle was appropriate protection for their black sheep, Irene—making the guard fit the crime. Or maybe he had been some lawyer's idea, about which the Crofts knew nothing. He could even have been a friend of the woman's, although I had trouble seeing her in a Vegas casino. Whoever was responsible for him, he was trouble I couldn't get around without bloodshed. Possibly my own blood.

It occurred to me that he wouldn't have been necessary unless someone—Irene or one of the more respectable Crofts—hadn't thought I could be a problem. Which might have meant that Irene was implicated in Robbie Segal's disappearance, though it seemed more likely that Clinger was implicated and that my investigation would link Irene to him and to the missing girl. So I'd been told to steer clear of Miss Irene, but Lavelle had not warned me away from Clinger. And that, I thought, was significant. It looked as if the Crofts had determined to throw Theo to the dogs, with the understanding that the family name wouldn't come up in the aftermath.

The more I thought about it, the more certain I became that that had been the meaning of the scene with Lavelle: stay away from Irene, and Clinger is your business. I still had to find him, with my best source of information blocked. But the situation was far from being hopeless. I could always try blonde Grace again or try to locate the boys in The Furies band. They seemed like my best bet. Grace knew who I was and what I was looking for, and she was tied to the Clinger family. It was smarter to hunt up some fresh faces, I thought, before going back to The Pentangle.

So I shifted the Pinto into gear and drove up Celestial to St. Gregory and then down to Hill. It took me about five minutes to find Corky's—a small, storefront bar halfway down the street with a neon Busch Beer sign blinking in the curtained window. The front door had been stopped open, and through it I could see the dark, rolled bar, gleaming with the red and blue lights of pinball machines. A couple of dozen wooden tables were arranged on the floor and what looked like a jerrybuilt stage was parked against the back wall. There was no one on the stage. I coasted down to the foot of Hill, parked beneath a budding hackberry, then walked back up to Corky's Bar.

I found an empty table just inside the door. While a pretty, blonde barmaid was getting me a beer, I took a leisurely look around. The place had begun to fill up a bit, which probably meant that showtime was near. I wondered who was performing and settled on a particularly large group of kids who were huddled around the tables next to the stage. It was hard to tell at that distance, since most of the light in Corky's was coming from neon beer signs and pinball machines, but I thought that I recognized one of them. A tall, skinny boy with shoulder-length blondish hair and a cool, imperious look on his face. I thought he was the same kid who had been holding a guitar in the photograph of Bobby and his two friends.

When the waitress came back with my beer, I asked her if she knew the kid's name.

She put a hand above her eyes, as if she were sighting down a fairway, and said, "That's Roger Tomilin. He plays rhythm guitar for The Furies. You ever heard them play?"

I shook my head.

"Well, stick around," she said. "They're on in about fifteen minutes."

"They're good, are they?" I asked her.

"They used to be. But their lead guitarist, Bobby, got himself killed a couple of days ago, and they're kind of shaken up about it. Plus, the guy they got to replace him isn't very good. That Bobby—he could really play."

She shook her head sadly and walked back to the bar. I turned in my chair and studied the youngsters gathered around the tables. There were ten of them—five boys dressed in T-shirts and jeans and five girls. One of the girls was sitting with her back to the group and staring glumly at the floorboards. She didn't look very old. None of them did, actually. But this one had a dimpled baby's face and curly brown hair that danced about her head like loose brass bedsprings. She was wearing a denim jacket, jeans, and hiking boots; and there was a nylon backpack at her feet. From the distraught look in her eyes, I figured she was trying to make up her mind about whether or not to leave the bar. Maybe she was thinking about leaving for good—the backpack looked full. The boy sitting beside her—a short, muscular twenty year old with a walrus moustache and long, jet-black hair—glanced at her jealously then turned to the rest of the group with a frown on his face that seemed to say that his girlfriend just wouldn't listen to reason. The four other boys seemed bored with his problems. Their minds were on the stage, where the house roadies were setting up amps and microphones. The girls seemed more sympathetic. They eyed the curly-haired girl hostilely, then looked at one another and shook their heads.

The throng in the bar continued to grow—a young, raucous crowd dressed like refugees and speaking a hoarse variety of tongues. From the look of their audience, The Furies were new wavers, which meant they weren't likely to have much use for a thirty-eight-year-old private detective in a sports coat. Especially if that detective started to ask them painful and embarrassing question about a murdered boy. Of course, they had been Bobby Caldwell's friends, and that counted for something. I just wasn't sure how much.

The roadies began to assemble the drum set, and that meant I didn't have much time to make up my mind about what to do. The boys would be on stage in five or ten minutes, and after that I'd have to take the chance of catching them between sets. I stared at them again. The girl with the curly hair was the one I really wanted to talk to. And it would be better still, I thought, if I could get her alone, away from her friends, where her mood might work to my advantage.

I glanced at the kids sitting around me, sucking on beer bottles and puffing cigarette smoke out into the room. Pinball machines had begun to thump and clang along the walls. And the crowd noise was growing very loud. In a few more minutes, the place would be roaring with guitars. I decided to go ahead and give The Furies a quick try, holding the curly-haired girl in reserve if I didn't get anywhere with the band.

I got up and worked my way across the room—tilting chairs back and apologizing to the kids sitting in them. A boy just missed spilling a pitcher of beer on my shoes. And I just missed running into a waitress. The whole room was beginning to smell like sour beer to me. I squeezed through the last obstacles—a couple of chairs placed back-to-back—and broke free right in front of the boy named Roger. He stared at me as if I were a clumsy drunk and said, "Get lost," in a squeaky tenor voice.

It was a bad beginning and I needed something to put me in command of the situation. So I reached into my coat, pulled out my wallet and flashed an old special deputy's badge in Roger's face. It looked official. And I wanted as much of his attention as I could get.

"He's a cop," one of the kids said to the girl sitting beside him.

"Aw, man," she said disgustedly.

"We already talked to the cops," Roger said.

But the noise was so loud that I didn't think I'd heard him right. "I want to ask you a few questions about Bobby Caldwell and Robbie Segal," I shouted over the din.

Roger shook his head and stood up. "What's the matter with you people?" he shouted back at me. "I just got done talking to a cop."

"When?" I said. "What cop?"

"Did you hear what he asked me?" Roger yelled to the kids at the table. "Talk about not getting your shit together!"

I looped my hand through his T-shirt and pulled him to within an inch of my face. His body went limp and his eyes clouded up sullenly.

162

"I asked you what cop and when?" I said between my teeth.

He turned his head away from mine. "A couple hours ago. I don't know his name. He had white hair and he pushed a lot harder than you do."

I let him go, and he fell back into his chair. "I still want to talk," I said.

"We got a set to do, man."

"Then afterwards," I said.

Roger said something very nasty under his breath and the rest of The Furies gave me ugly looks. Things were not working out the way I'd wanted them to. But then I'd chosen to act the part of a tough cop, thinking it would give me leverage with a bunch of punk rockers. If I had known that Bannock had been there before me, I would have taken a more sympathetic role. I should have called the son-of-a-bitch like I'd planned to do, I thought.

I glanced down at the curly-haired girl, but she was scowling at me, too. Great, I said to myself.

Someone on stage yelled at Roger, and he said, "All right."

He looked at me as if he were asking my permission to start the show. I nodded and the band got up. While they were tuning their instruments, I slunk back to my seat, sat down, and stared miserably at my glass of beer. Someone had dropped a cigarette in it—which pretty much summed up the way things were going for me that night. I felt like crawling out of the bar. Instead, I leaned an elbow on the tabletop and pretended to listen to The Furies, who proved to be very loud and not very good. They butchered "Satisfaction," then began to work on an old blues song.

163

I was thinking vaguely about Bannock—wondering how he'd gotten to the band before I had and wondering stupidly why he'd gotten rough with them—when I noticed the curly-haired girl picking up her backpack. She walked toward the rear of the bar. As soon as she'd cleared the door, I got up and followed her.

It was close to nine o'clock and Hill Street had begun to jump. Bar doors were open up and down the street, filling the sidewalks with noise. The pedestrian traffic was fairly heavy, too. I pushed my way through it, trailing the girl as she walked north up Hill into the dark, residential side streets at the top of Mt. Adams. She was a fast walker, so it took me a couple of minutes to catch up to her. By then we were on Hatch Street, where the only lights came from gas lamps and the only noise was the sound of our footsteps on the pavement. When I got abreast of her, she glanced at me, then lowered her head like a bulldog and stepped up her pace.

"I haven't broken any laws, have I?" she said as we jogged along.

"No," I said hoarsely. Hill Street had been a forty-degree grade, and the girl was practically running.

"Then I don't have to talk to you," she said.

"It's about Bobby Caldwell," I panted.

"I heard in the bar."

"Yeah, but I'm not really a cop. I'm a private detective hired by the mother of Bobby's girlfriend."

She eyed me suspiciously. "Why didn't you tell Roger that?"

"I don't know," I admitted. "Judging by his looks, I didn't think it would mean much to him."

"You thought right," she said with a bitter laugh.

164

She began to slow down a bit. Which was a very good thing, because my legs were starting to give out.

"You're not in very good shape for a detective," she said acidly.

"I'm not eighteen years old, either," I said.

"Nineteen," she said with a touch of defiance. "I'm nineteen years old."

"I'm thirty-eight," I said as if it were a kind of greeting.

She thought things over for a second, then stopped so abruptly that I walked past her. She stared at me while I tried to catch my breath.

"Are you really a private detective?"

I pulled my I.D. out of my pocket and handed it to her.

"And you're working for Robbie's mother?" she said.

"You know Robbie?" I asked her.

The girl nodded. "I know her," she said.

"Do you know where she is? Her mother's going crazy with worry."

"Her mother's a first-class bitch," the girl said.

I wanted to say something in Mildred's defense but knew it was the wrong approach to take with this girl. So I ended up saying, "She cares about Robbie. Enough to have hired me to find her."

"And what will you do—if you find her?"

I told her the truth. "I'll take her home." The girl gave me a searching look and I added: "I'll take her home whether she wants to come or not, if that's what you're wondering."

Apparently it was exactly what she'd been wondering, because her face closed up like a dent in dough. "I don't know," she said slowly.

"If I were in your position, I wouldn't know either," I said. "As it is, I've had to think about it myself—a couple

165

of times. Runaway cases aren't much fun for anyone."

She almost smiled. "I think you must be a lousy detective," she said, handing my I.D. back.

"Actually I'm a very good detective. This is just a lousy case."

She looked around us, at the dark, silent brownstones on Hatch Street. "Do you have a car?"

I told her I did.

"Would you give me a ride some place?"

"Sure."

She adjusted one of the straps on her backpack and said, "This is kind of heavy, and I want to make it to the bus station by ten."

"You're leaving town?"

"I'm leaving," she said a bit guardedly, as if she didn't want to be asked why.

"Well, come on, then," I said. "I'm parked down the street."

She took another quick look at me, decided I was all right, and started walking back down to Hill. "My name's Annie," she said.

"Mine's Harry."

"Pleased to meet you," she said.

20

IT TOOK US FIVE MINUTES TO GET TO THE CAR AND another ten to drive over to the Greyhound Bus Station on lower Gilbert Avenue. By the time we got there, Annie had begun to warm up a little. But just a little; she still wasn't sure of me. I wasn't sure of me, either, or of why I'd decided to give her a lift. But things had been going badly that night; and if nothing else, helping the girl had given me the chance to act like a decent human being again. Of course, it also gave me the chance to learn something more about Robbie, although I didn't do any pushing with this one. I felt as if I'd done enough pushing in Corky's Bar.

When we got inside the depot, I took Annie to the coffee shop and boosted her to a Coke. The place looked like early morning in an all-night diner. It was just a quarter of ten, but the waitress was already droopy-eyed and sluggish. A handful of seedy, worn-out men were gathered around the counter, hunched miserably over coffee cups and crumpled Racing Forms. Annie and I were the only couple in the joint.

A few of the men eyed the girl hungrily as we sat

down. I could feel her shiver and tighten up. She was a smart, independent young lady, but she was no match for the Greyhound Bus Station. I wondered what she was doing there—where she had come from and where she was going—but I didn't ask. From the beaten look of her backpack, I could see she'd been on the road before. And when she reached for the Coke, I caught a glimpse of a half-moon tattoo on her right wrist—the sort of thing that bikers' girls decorated themselves with. She certainly didn't sound like a motorcycle queen. She seemed to be a very intelligent kid. She might even have gone to college for a quarter or two before dropping out—like Grace. But she wasn't as cocky as Grace had been. Or as slick and venal. She still had a kind of rough, styleless edge to her, as if she hadn't yet settled on the type of woman she wanted to be. But then she was only nineteen, and that rough, inchoate quality suited her.

She drank her Coke and when I got up to pay the bill, she said, "Would you mind waiting here with me until the bus comes? I almost got raped in a bus station once, and this place gives me the creeps."

I told her I'd stay.

We wandered out of the coffee shop to the waiting area and sat down on a couple of hard plastic chairs. There was only a smattering of people waiting with us, and half of them looked as if they'd come inside to nod off. It was cheaper than a flop house.

We sat there watching the arrival times flash on a closed-circuit TV. When a P.A. announcer said that the bus to Denver would be delayed ten minutes, Annie sighed.

"That means half an hour," she said unhappily.

"You're going to Denver?"

168

She nodded. "I'm going as far away as seventy bucks will take me."

"Why?" I said. I felt as if I could say it now, without sounding like a detective.

"Things," she said gravely. "It was just a bad scene where I was living. Very bad."

"You mean the kid with the moustache?"

"Larry?" she said with a laugh. "No, I wasn't living with Larry. He might have thought I was, but I wasn't. I was living with a bunch of people on a farm." Annie sighed heavily. "For a while, it was beautiful." She glanced at me guiltily, as if she'd revealed something about herself that she didn't want known, then she looked down at the concrete floor and sighed again. "I guess I better tell you a couple things," she said in a soft, sad voice. "Roger told the cop most of it anyway, so I guess I can tell you, too."

"What things?"

"It's about Robbie. This farm I was at—she was staying there, too. At least she was four days ago."

And there it was. What I'd been looking for since Wednesday afternoon.

I felt as if I'd wandered into it by mistake, although when I thought of the photograph of Roger and Bobby and the other musician, I realized that it was perfectly reasonable. I'd thought that all three of them had been visiting the farm for the day, when the truth was that Bobby had been the only visitor. The Furies and their girls had apparently lived there as part of Clinger's family.

"Robbie was at the farm on Tuesday?" I said to Annie.

"Yes. She came in on Sunday night. Bobby dropped her off."

169

"He didn't stay with her?" I said with surprise.

"I think he wanted to stay," the girl said. "But Theo acted like he was being too protective. Theo said she had to learn to survive on her own." Annie looked down at the floor. "That's the same thing he said when anyone new came to the farm."

I could tell from her voice that she was speaking for herself, as well as for Robbie, and that she was speaking out of a deeply felt sense of disillusionment. It wasn't a resentful feeling, if I was hearing her right. It was more wintry than that, as if something she'd once loved dearly had turned out terribly wrong. I decided to be completely honest with her, because I wanted to follow that line of feeling to its source. I wanted to know who or what had gone so wrong.

"Annie, I know who Clinger is," I said. "I've been trying to locate him for the last few days." I took the photograph of Robbie, Irene, and Clinger out of my coat and showed it to her.

The girl winced when she saw the picture. For some reason, the sudden look of pain on her face frightened me.

"She's the one," the girl said in a haggard voice. "She's the reason." She tapped the photograph and handed it back to me. I couldn't tell whom she'd pointed to—Robbie or Irene—although I was almost certain it was the Croft woman.

"The reason for what?" I asked her.

But she went on as if she hadn't heard the question. "Man, it was so beautiful at the start. I've bounced around since I left Detroit and seen some things, but when I got there, I thought, 'This is it, Annie. This is what you've been looking for!' You just can't know what it was

170

like—to find a place like Theo's farm, where no one seemed to care about all the shit things you're supposed to care about. I mean, it was too good to be true. I almost didn't believe it myself. When you've been fucked over by everyone from your boyfriend to your old man, you get that way. You figure it's another gimmick—another way to get you to slip your pants off. But Theo's farm . . . it wasn't like that. I mean, you could do it if you wanted to. Practically everybody did. But you didn't have to do it. Nobody beat you up or locked you in your room or threatened to kill you if you didn't come across. You had to work, of course. Earn your keep. But you didn't have to fuck unless you wanted to. And you *did* want to, because it seemed like the best way to be. It was like, instead of money and rules and all the crap you're taught in school, we had love. I know that sounds old. But that was the way it felt. Like love was the real way to pay and to be repaid. And I don't mean sex. I mean love."

Annie's eyes filled with tears. "Theo, man," she said. "He was so good. He was so deep. It was as if there wasn't anything he hadn't done. Not a thing he didn't know about. He understood it all. He'd been there before you, and he'd forgiven them for you. My fucking old man. My mother who watched the TV and drank and didn't give a shit about anything but the neighbors. He understood them. He could love them—so goddamn unlovable. And what I don't understand"—she began to cry—"is what went wrong, man? How could it all get so fucked up?"

She sobbed heavily. I put my arm around her shoulder, and she fell against my chest. My heart went out to her —for all that she'd lost. After awhile, Annie stopped crying and just sat there with her cheek buried in my coat.

"I don't know what I'm going to do," she said. "I've never been to Denver."

"It's a beautiful city," I said.

She nodded against my chest. "Beautiful," she said.

"Are you going to be O.K.?" I asked her after another minute.

"Yeah." She lifted her head from my shoulder and wiped her eyes on her coat sleeve. "I'm all right," she said. "I'm a lot tougher than I look."

The P.A. came on with a pop that made us both jump. The announcer said that the bus to St. Louis, Kansas City, and Denver was arriving at dock ten.

Annie reached down and picked up her beaten backpack. She studied it for a moment, then heaved it over her shoulder and stood up.

"Walk me to the loading dock?" she said.

I got up and guided her across the huge concrete plaza to the loading docks.

"Robbie was at the farm on Monday and Tuesday," she said as we walked. "I don't know if she's still there or not. Bobby didn't want her to stay. They had a big fight about it on Tuesday night—Theo, Bob, and Robbie. It got very ugly. Bob was furious because Robbie wouldn't come away with him. I think he blamed Theo for that. But then there had been so much arguing and shouting over the last few weeks that I didn't pay much attention to what was said. I'd already decided to go myself. I left that night. So did some of the others."

"You don't know what the argument was about?" I said.

"Bob didn't want her to stay at the farm any more. He didn't want her fucking around."

"Was she?"

Annie didn't answer me for a moment. "Robbie wasn't like the rest of us," she finally said. "She just hadn't been around very much. She'd spent her whole life in one room, and I guess when she got out, she went a little crazy. It was too much for her, I think. Being able to do whatever she wanted to do. And the weird thing was that she didn't really understand what she was doing to Bob and to the rest of us. She was just too young to understand. I guess it's hard to be that beautiful and that young. It's as if the two don't go together right."

When we got to the loading dock, I asked her, "What went wrong, Annie? Why are you leaving?"

She bit her lip and glanced at the bus door. Six people were standing in line, while the driver took their tickets and checked their luggage.

"I guess I can tell you. Roger told the cop. So I guess I can tell you. It was money. Theo got in over his head on a couple of deals. And things got very bad. At first we thought it was going to be all right—that he'd gotten some help. But then a couple of weeks ago some men came out to the farm—guys in business suits. I think they would have killed Theo if we hadn't been there. It was a real desperate scene."

I said, "What kind of deals was Theo involved in, Annie?"

She shook her head, as if she didn't want to say.

"Was it drugs, Annie?"

She made a sad face and nodded.

I felt another twinge of fear—for the girl in front of me and for Robbie. "Where's the farm, Annie? How can I find it?"

"Oh, Harry," she said brokenly. "Please don't ask me

173

that. Ask Roger or ask the cops. They know. But don't ask me."

"I don't have time to ask Roger, Annie. You know that."

"But Theo!" she cried. "What'll happen to Theo?"

"All I'm interested in is Robbie," I told her. "I want her to get away, too. Before it's too late."

She hung her head on her chest and whispered, "Across the river. On Route 4, about five miles west of Anderson Ferry."

She turned on her heel and ran to the bus.

"Annie!" I called out.

But she was already inside. The door hissed shut and the bus began to pull out of the dock. I watched it go and kept watching it until the taillights disappeared down Gilbert Avenue.

21

I TRIED CALLING BANNOCK FROM A PAY PHONE IN THE
Greyhound coffee shop, but the duty sergeant at Central
Station told me he'd already checked out. I suppose it
should have made me feel better to know that Bannock
—who had the same information that I had or, at least,
most of it—had felt as if he could put the case away for
the night. Only it didn't make me feel better. Bannock
had been investigating Bobby Caldwell's murder, and
he'd ended up in the same place I had. I didn't like that
one bit. I hadn't liked what I'd heard from Annie, either.
She'd been badly frightened by what had been happening at Clinger's farm—so frightened that she'd decided
to run as far away as she could go. There was definitely
a great deal of trouble in paradise, and although Robbie
didn't seem to be directly involved in it, she was still
living there—or she had been up until Tuesday night.
And after Bobby's murder on Wednesday, she'd had no
way out, except Annie's way. And judging by what I'd
heard that evening, Robbie wasn't old enough or experienced enough to have made an escape of her own,
even if she'd wanted to.

175

I put the phone back on its hook and glanced at my watch. It was ten-thirty. If I stepped on it, I figured I could make it to the Anderson Ferry marina by eleven and then over to the Kentucky side. Only it would be hell trying to locate Clinger's farm in the middle of the night. At least in the daylight I'd have an even chance of spotting a familiar face or of finding a helpful neighbor. But after talking to Annie, I just couldn't see waiting another day. It had been too long for Annie to wait, and she'd had most of the week to think it over. I thought of the look on her face when I'd shown her the picture of Robbie, Clinger, and Irene Croft. She'd blamed the Croft woman for what had gone wrong out there—I was almost sure of it. And if Irene was that deeply involved in Clinger's family, she was one more reason to bring Robbie out as quickly as I could—a particularly ugly reason from what I'd seen of her.

Her presence at the farm certainly made better sense if Clinger had been involved in the drug trade, as Annie had said. Marcie had told me that Irene was a druggie, and the whole world knew that she was a very rich and very eccentric lady. Clinger might have needed her backing to finance a particularly large deal. I had no idea how he'd rationalized the addition of someone that hard and loveless to his family of love, but I figured he might have managed it, and the demands she'd made on his talent, in return for a sizable loan. And Irene would probably have been delighted to acquire a talented new client and a free supply of cocaine or smack or whatever else it was that Clinger had been hustling. She might even have gotten her pick of Clinger's followers as part of the arrangement. It would have been a swell deal for both of them, if something hadn't gone wrong. Perhaps

176

Irene had backed out at the last moment, or maybe Clinger had just gotten in over both of their heads. In any event, he'd come up short. But I figured he'd been coming up short for a long time. Maybe inflation and tight money had forced him into drug trafficking in the first place, as a way of keeping the rest of his empire afloat. There was no telling what risks he might have run to maintain the illusion that love, not money, was the true source of his power. Whatever had gone awry, he'd had that illusion beaten out of him by some mob toughs. And when his illusions gave out, the whole enterprise had begun to collapse like a ruined kingdom.

Annie had gotten out before the end. Maybe the rest of The Furies had gotten out, too. But I had the strong feeling that Theo Clinger was going to take whoever else was left out at the farm with him when he fell. As I walked out of the bus station to the parking lot, I couldn't help thinking that one of his luckless followers had already been sacrificed.

There really wasn't any way around it. Bobby's murder had to be linked to what had been going on at the farm. There was just no other way to make sense of it. What Annie had told me about the fight the boy had had with Clinger on Tuesday night and the fact that Arthur Bannock was investigating Theo, too, clinched it for me. The Caldwell boy must have gotten in the way. He must have made someone very, very angry. Someone who had no patience or pity left. Someone who'd wanted to watch him die.

And that was another reason why I couldn't wait for the daylight. I started the Pinto up and headed west, through the Third Street basin to River Road.

It was a little after eleven when I turned off Highway 52 onto the bumpy dirt lane that led to the Anderson Ferry marina. A thin, river-dwelling fog hung above the dock. It swirled like mist around my feet as I got out of the car and walked over to the landing. The ferry wasn't moored on the Ohio side of the river, but there was a rusted signal bell hung from one of the piles. I slapped my arms against the cold night air and pulled the bell cord. The bell clanged dully, as if I'd knocked it off a shelf, and a few seconds later an answering bell sounded across the foggy water. A power winch began to putt and cough like a lawnmower, and I could hear the rustle and splash of the towline as it tautened and leaped out of the river. I walked back to the car and leaned against the hood. The night had turned so cold that the hood metal bit through my trouser leg, making me shiver.

In a matter of minutes, I could make out the water lights of the ferryboat, as it guided its flat barge up to the dock. The wheelhouse was lit by an oil lamp. I could see the helmsman inside it, passing his hands nimbly over the wheel. As the boat got closer, I could see another man standing on the barge's deck. He leaped onto the landing as the boat docked and threw a line over one of the pilings.

"Well, c'mon," he shouted to me.

He had a young, exuberant voice.

I drove the Pinto onto the barge, and the boy cast off the line and hopped back on deck. The winch started up again with a shudder, and the ferryboat began to chug its way back through the fog to the Kentucky shore.

The boy sat down on the barge rail and began to whis-tle tunelessly. He had a country boy's red, lumpy face. He was wearing a watch cap and windbreaker. I got out

178

of the car and let the damp wind sober me up. It was getting late, and I had a long night ahead of me. The smell of hot coffee drifting out of the wheelhouse made my mouth water.

"You know if there's an all-night diner close by?" I said to the deckhand.

"One about two miles up Route 4, going west," he said. "Tillie's Diner. She makes good pecan pie, too."

"I'll remember that," I said.

The boy swiped at the fog as if it were a swarm of gnats floating in front of his face. "Bad night," he said.

I nodded. "You know the Kentucky side of the river pretty well?"

"Pretty well," he said.

"You know a guy named Clinger who owns a farm about five miles west of here? I'm trying to find his place."

The boy shook his head. "Don't know him. But you might ask at Tillie's. She knows just about everybody 'round here."

The boat docked with a lurch.

"Damn," the kid said, glancing at the wheelhouse.

He jumped off the rail and onto the landing and made the boat fast again.

As I got out of the car, I heard him say to the helmsman, "You might give us a little warning, Willie."

I coasted off onto the dock, handed the kid a couple of dollars, and drove up a short hill out of the fog. The road led through a grove of sycamores and ended abruptly in a gravel turnaround on the north side of Route 4. I turned right onto the two-lane highway and headed west for Tillie's.

For a mile or so, the sycamores grew thick on the river

179

side of the road. My headlights played among their trunks, lighting up the rusty marine refuse scattered on the ground and the fiery red eyes of opossums. On the south side of the roadbed, the Kentucky hills rose in a steep plane that blocked out most of the night sky.

I kept driving west. And eventually the sycamores died off and I could see the fogbound river again and the pinpoint lights of the shanties built above the bank. Then the highway jogged south into the hillside. As it moved inland, Route 4 took on a civil, neighborly look. Historical markers popped up on the north side of the road. So did white slat gas stations and shed restaurants and glassed-in motel offices with tiny stucco bungalows herded behind them like grazing sheep. Tillie's Diner was just another shed on the roadside, with corrugated tin roof and walls. But its lights were still on and its sign read, "Open All Night."

I pulled into the lot and parked beside a semi. There were half a dozen big trucks in the lot. According to folklore, that meant Tillie served good food. But I had the feeling it meant that Tillie's was the only place that stayed open for about forty miles in either direction. The restaurant looked like a pint-sized airplane hanger with a plantation porch. I walked through the door, past a glass display case full of aviator sunglasses and penknives and key chains shaped like Kentucky, and sat down at a long, U-shaped counter.

A meaty, heavily made-up woman with orange hair and a wart the size of a button mushroom under her nose was sitting on a stool behind the counter, reading a copy of *Glamour* magazine. She had on a green plastic waitress' uniform, a gold bracelet, and silver earrings with red stones in them. She put the magazine down when

180

she spotted me, pulled a pencil from behind her ear, and ambled up to the counter.

"What'll it be, honey?" she said in a sweet, nasal voice. She smelled like lilacs and bourbon.

"Just coffee," I said.

She pulled a cup out from beneath the counter and set it down before me. Then she got a percolator off a hot-plate and poured coffee into the cup.

"Are you Tillie?" I asked her as she poured the coffee.

"Yes, I am, honey. Been Tillie all my life."

"The guy at the Anderson Ferry told me you might be able to help me."

"Well, now, that depends on what kind of help you need," she said slyly.

I grinned at her. "I'm looking for a farm near here, owned by a fella' named Clinger. Theo Clinger. You think you could help me find it?"

"You all a friend of Theo's?" she said.

"I'm his cousin," I told her.

Tillie threw her hand at me playfully. "You ain't his cousin. You don't look a bit like Theo."

"What difference does it make? I still want to find him."

"No difference to me, honey," she said carelessly. "That Theo sure is a popular fella all of a sudden, though. You're the second one tonight come in wanting to find his farm."

"Was the first guy a short, stocky man with white hair?" I asked her.

She nodded. "You ain't *his* cousin too, are you?"

I shook my head. "I'm his son."

Tillie barked with laughter. "Well, I'll tell you what I told your old man. You go on up Route 4 a little over two

181

miles until you come to a fenced-in cornfield on the south side of the road. They'll be a sign on the gate saying, 'Private Property.' Just go on through that gate up the road 'bout half a mile and you'll come to Theo's farmhouse. But don't you let on that I sent you, hear?"

"I won't," I promised. "When did you say my father stopped in?"

"I didn't say, honey. But it was around seven o'clock this evening."

I swallowed the rest of the coffee, dug a couple of dollars out of my pocket, and laid them on the counter. "Thanks, Tillie," I said.

She shook her head with rueful amusement. "You cops kill me."

"What makes you think I'm a cop?"

"The size of the tip for one. And for two, who else comes visiting at twelve o'clock at night and don't have no idea how to get where he wants to go?"

When I thought about it, she had a point.

22

HAD NO TROUBLE FINDING THE FARM. IT WAS EXACTLY where Tillie had said it would be, two and a half miles up Route 4 on the south side of the highway—a fenced-in field with a lumpy dirt access road cutting through it like a keloid scar. I pulled the Pinto off the highway and parked in front of the gate. Somewhere, farther down the road, a hound began to bay forlornly. His broken, querulous voice carried across the dark field like the peal of a warning bell. And then, as suddenly as it had begun, the baying stopped, and the roadside was filled with a cottony quiet, like the hush at the heart of a pine forest on a cold January day.

I couldn't see a farmhouse from where I was sitting. The field appeared to rise steeply for a couple hundred yards before falling away into a glen or valley on its south slope. The farmhouse was probably located in the hollow —invisible from the roadside. I stared at the rusted tin sign posted on the gate—*Private Property*.

I wondered for a moment whether I could pull the same trick on Clinger that I'd pulled on his disciple, Roger—claim that I was a cop and flash the Special

Deputy's badge at him. That might get me onto the porch. But it sure wouldn't get me in the front door, not if Clinger was in the kind of trouble I thought he was in. If he was involved in the drug trade, even a cop would need a search warrant to get inside the house—I was sure of that. Moreover, he was bound to be suspicious and edgy, especially if Bannock had paid him a visit earlier that night. The smart thing to do would be to try calling Bannock again, I thought, and to find out exactly what he was onto.

I toyed with the idea of driving back to Tillie's Diner and phoning the cops, but I was already there, within shouting distance of Robbie Segal. And I didn't want to leave without making that shout. Oddly enough I felt fairly certain the girl was still alive. Which wasn't to say that I didn't feel Robbie wasn't in danger. Just that I couldn't see her following Bobby to the grave, like a spring widow. In the light of what I'd learned, the two of them now seemed like protagonists in different stories —the devoted lover of a medieval romance and the impetuous heroine of a gothic adventure story. It was an ill-formed match—but I'd sensed that all along. What I hadn't realized, until I'd talked to Annie, was just how hopeless Bobby's love had been from the start. I wondered now if the girl had ever loved the boy or if, like her mother, she never understood what the word meant.

She had maneuvered Bobby into taking her to paradise—to a world that he and a lot of other people had thought of as being constituted solely of love. And she'd grown fast to the place, like one of those fleeing women in mythology turned into a brook. She'd become part of Clinger's world, so immediately and so completely that she'd astonished Annie and the Caldwell boy with the

184

very fierceness of her attachment. Annie had seen some-thing inexplicable in that attachment. But then she hadn't been following the girl as I had—hadn't seen the loveless street she'd come from or been in her antiseptic room and seen the paltry dream she'd concocted there out of a few icons and a few paragraphs in a book, like a bird made of paste and newsprint. And then Robbie was very young, as Annie had said, and very beautiful, which is a cruel combination, as all precocity is cruel.

I sat there trying to excuse the runaway girl of blame, and suddenly realized that I was in the same position that Bobby Caldwell had been in—that instead of ex-plaining the girl, I'd ended up explaining him. Sitting there, in the dead midnight, I felt as if I'd been retracing his steps all along, right up until that very moment, as I prepared to make my own attempt at rescuing a girl who didn't seem to know how lost she had become. Maybe she could explain herself, I thought, when I finally found her.

I flipped on the inside light, opened the glove com-partment, and took out a pair of binoculars, a flashlight, and a flask of Scotch. The special deputy approach was useless, I decided. Any direct approach was useless if the girl didn't want to cooperate. And if she hadn't gone away with Bobby, there was no reason to think she'd come out with me. Or that Clinger would even let me try to persuade her to come. Followers must have been getting hard to come by for Theo, and those that were left had to be hard-core fanatics. What I wanted to do was to case the farm from a distance, trying to spot the girl or, if I was really lucky, to catch her there alone. Or virtually alone. Then I'd either take her out by force or I'd sit on the place until the chance to grab her came up.

It was little better than a kidnapping, but I couldn't see any other way to bring her out.

I flipped off the car light and opened the door. Before stepping outside, I reached under the dash and pulled the Colt Gold Cup from the pistol rack. I checked the magazine, cocked the piece, locked it, and stuck it firmly in my belt. Then I strapped the binoculars around my neck, stuck the flashlight and the flask in my coat pockets, and walked into the night.

The open, fallow field provided no brake against the wind, which was running down the hillside like an ice floe. I was cold through and through by the time I reached the crest of the hill. I turned my back to the wind, sat down in one of the furrows, and pulled the flask out of my coat. The liquor brought tears to my eyes, cleared my nose, and unblocked my ears. And suddenly I could smell the damp earth all around me and hear the wind whistling across the barren field.

I took a quick look at the Pinto—parked beside the gate—then turned around and trained the binoculars on the south slope. The field was plowed for sowing for another hundred yards. Then it died away in a muddy swale full of day lilies and tall green rushes. Beyond the marsh, lilacs were planted in a row, their grape-like flowers glowing like blue velvet in the night. And beyond the hedge row, the tall, irregular silhouette of a farm house and a barn and a silo rose out of the earth like a nighttime shadow.

I swept the binoculars across the farm yard, where daffodils clustered in the dirt. There weren't any signs of life—in the yard or in the house or in the outbuildings. No lamplights. No glowing cigarettes. No parked cars or farm machinery. And no sound, except for the wind. I glanced at my watch, which was showing a quarter of one, and thought that the Clinger family had either gone to sleep or gone out for the night. I looked back at the Pinto, as if it were a warm, inviting bed. But the chance of having that farmhouse to myself was too good to pass by. I got back to my feet and started down the hill.

I skirted the muddy swale at the edge of the yard and came out behind the barn, on the eastern side of the farm. There was a window set in the barn's rear wall. I shined the flashlight through it and peered in. A tractor was parked in the middle of the floor, between two rows of feed stalls, but there weren't any cars inside or any fresh tire tracks in the dust. Which made it that much more likely that there was no one at home. I clicked off the light and slid around to the front of the barn. The farmhouse was about twenty yards from the outbuildings, facing northwest toward the access road. When I was satisfied that there really wasn't anybody else around, I scampered across the open ground to the rear porch. A compressor was throbbing dully nearby. I hadn't heard it until I'd gotten to the back of the house. I figured it was located at the base of one of the walls, lying in the grass like an overturned water tank. The fact that it was still running made me feel better, because, from the deserted look of things, I'd been wondering whether Clinger hadn't flown the coop altogether.

The rear porch was just a concrete abutment, leading to a screened wooden door. I walked up the steps and tried the handle, but it was locked tight. There were two windows on either side of the door, only they were both closed and they were both too far off the ground and too far from the rear stoop to be jimmied. I examined the

187

door again, pulled a credit card from my wallet, and tried to force the lock. I almost broke my Mastercard in two. The latch was a deadbolt—impossible to open without a hacksaw or a set of files or a key. That left the front door and windows.

I climbed back down the steps and walked around the north side of the house to the front yard. The aluminum windows in the north wall were screened and latched. The whole house had been freshly sided in aluminum strips and painted the mealy color of cornbread. The renovations must have cost Clinger a bundle; but then I figured they'd probably been done in the good old days before money problems had forced him into the drug business.

There was an apple tree planted in the front lawn with clumps of sedge scattered like cabbage leaves around its trunk. I stared at the tree for a moment before turning the corner. I knew what I'd find in front—I guess that was why I paused. And it was there, all right, when I finally stepped into the yard—the wooden porch with its six steps and its railed landing. I'd been looking at a photograph of it for four days, and seeing it in reality unnerved me—filled me with an eerie sense of déjà vu, as if I'd actually been there before. I carried that feeling with me up the stairs onto the dark landing. Another half-step led to the front door. There were two storm windows flanking it.

I tried the door handle and was about to try the left window when I heard a footstep on the stairs behind me. The sound sent a chill up my spine.

"Wha'chu doing, fella?" a man's soft, mocking voice said.

"Trying to get in," I said meekly. And then I put a little iron in my voice and added: "I'm a cop."

188

"Sure you are," the laughing voice replied.

"I've got I.D.," I said quickly, but when I reached for my coat pocket, I let my right hand drop onto the cold butt of the pistol. My Special Deputy's badge wasn't going to fool this one—I could hear that in his voice.

"You best put your hands above your head," the man said. "I'd hate to shoot an officer of the law."

"You've got a gun?" I said stupidly.

"A Remington pump. And it's pointed at the back of your head."

"I don't suppose we could talk this over?"

He laughed. "You just raise your hands."

I slipped the gun from my belt and started to raise my arms.

"Higher!" the man said with sudden sharpness.

I had about five seconds to decide what to do. If I dropped the pistol and went along with him, there was a chance I could talk my way out of it. But I figured it would have to be some mighty straight talk—the kind that would blow any chance of getting the girl out quietly, although I knew that chance might already have been blown.

I shifted my eyes to the left and looked at the porch rail. It was about a step and a half from where I was standing, and it was low enough that I could vault it easily. I didn't want to shoot anyone, but I didn't want to put myself at the mercy of one of Clinger's followers, either. Mercy didn't appear to be their strong suit.

"I'm not fucking with you, mister," the man said. "Either you raise your arms or you're going to be tasting your own brains."

"I'm moving," I said and jumped for the rail.

The shotgun went off behind me with a terrific bang. The left front window exploded in a hail of glass and splintered aluminum. I could hear the pellets spattering through the house, breaking glass and slamming into furniture with dull, concussive thuds. But I was over the rail by then.

I hadn't counted on the drop. It was a good six and a half feet from the porch rail to the yard, and I landed badly, twisting my left ankle in a nest of sedge and rock. I was still trying to pick myself up when the man came ambling around the corner. I didn't even have the pistol unlocked. I heard him pull the pump back and knew that if I pointed the gun at him I'd be dead.

"All right," I said. "All right."

I tossed the Colt on the ground. I could see the man smile. His teeth and his eyes and the gun barrel were about the only things I could see in the darkness.

"Kick it on out here," he said.

I kicked the gun away from me and stared at it for a second, lying in the sedge. Then I got to my feet, leaned back against the wall, and dusted some of the dirt off my pants leg. My ankle was beginning to throb and burn. I wouldn't be able to run on it—or, at least, not very far. I watched the man as he walked up to me. He was wearing a leather flyer's jacket and jeans, and he looked more like a bodyguard than one of Clinger's followers. I figured that was probably what he was—hired muscle, like Jerry Lavelle. Only this one was the local variety. A young, brainless Kentucky thug.

"Hurt yourself, did you?" he said with a generous smile.

"My ankle."

He nodded and slapped the shotgun barrel across the right side of my head. He hit me so quickly and so hard that my skull bounced against the aluminum siding of the farmhouse. I think the only thing that kept me standing on my feet was sheer surprise. I touched my temple and felt the blood running down my cheek. Then I stared goofily at the man standing in front of me. He was still smiling.

Back to the wall, I slipped to the ground and sat there —legs stretched out in front of me—looking at the pattern my blood had made in the dirt. Someone else came up beside me, but I blacked out before I could lift my head to look at him.

23

WHEN I WOKE UP I DIDN'T KNOW WHERE I WAS OR WHAT had happened to me. I could hear someone playing a piano—toying with it like a kid practicing the scales. And there was a bright light overhead. It made me wince when I opened my eyes. Then I remembered that I'd been hurt and touched gingerly at the right side of my head. Something inside my skull throbbed like an infected tooth.

I groaned aloud and the sound of the piano stopped.

It took me a few seconds, but I managed to sit up. I was on a couch—an old Victorian number with velvet cushions and a dark, glossy wooden frame. I stared dully at the carpeted floor and waited for my mind to clear. Judging by the pain in my head, the blurred vision, and the faint nausea I was feeling, I figured I'd suffered a concussion.

I rested my head against the cushion and watched the room come into focus: a small parlor, with white plastered walls and second-hand Victorian furnishings. There was an upright piano on the wall across from the couch, and a man was sitting in front of it, with his back to me. He ran his fingers down the keyboard and turned around. I thought I knew his face.

"Clinger?" I said.

The man nodded. "I'm Theo Clinger."

He stared at me intently, as he'd stared into the camera in the photograph. He had long black hair, streaked with gray, and black, heavy-lidded, vaguely oriental eyes. The rest of his face was thin, fleshless, and as white as bone. Even his lips were whitish. His dark eyes looked like the lumps of coal in a snowman's head.

"Where am I?" I said to the snowman.

"You're at my farm. In the house."

I suddenly remembered the man with the shotgun and how I'd been hurt. I asked Clinger why the man had hit me and he laughed.

"You were trying to break in. And we've had some trouble lately. The only reason you're not lying in a ditch right now is that you have a friend here who told us who you were."

Robbie's name popped into my head and I spoke it.

"She's not here," Clinger said. "She left with Bobby on Wednesday."

"Bobby?" I said stupidly. I wanted to ask him about Bobby, but for a moment I couldn't think of what to say. "What happened to Bobby?"

Clinger tapped his fingertips together and considered the question. "I'm going to be honest with you. I know who you are and who you're looking for. And I don't want any trouble with the law. Bobby took Robbie with him when he left here on Wednesday. That was the last time I saw either one of them."

"What happened to him?" I said again.

My head was clearing and I was beginning to get a

193

sharper sense of the man in front of me. He had a cool, candid, melancholy voice that didn't quite match the arrogant, fleshless face. I wondered vaguely if he was putting on the candor for me or if he always spoke in that sad, considered way.

"I believe Bobby was killed by my enemies," he finally said. "I've already told the police this earlier tonight. I see no reason not to tell you. A lot of people don't understand where we're coming from here at the farm. They don't approve of our lifestyle, and they express their disapproval in violent ways—poisoning our wells and our livestock. I believe Bobby was killed by some of them, as a warning to me."

"You're telling me he was lynched?" I said incredulously.

"He may have been," Clinger said. "I've had business dealings with some of these people. It's quite easy to feel cheated by someone you don't like—someone you're afraid of, someone whose values you don't agree with. A few of these men came out to the farm a couple of weeks ago. They threatened my life and the lives of my family. That's the reason why I hired Logan and his friend."

I made a confused face and Clinger pointed to my head.

"Logan is the man who found you on the porch."

"I see."

I wanted to ask him about what Annie had told me—about the drug connection. He'd made it seem as if the business he'd been involved in was perfectly ordinary and that the men had come after him because they hadn't liked his looks. Perhaps that was the way he'd rationalized it—as one more foray from the straight world, aimed at destroying his unconventional empire.

194

After twenty years of hippiedom, it would be fairly easy to see the world in black and white. But rationalizations aside, he was hedging. Drug dealers weren't ordinary businessmen, and they weren't straight arrows, either. What he wasn't saying made the rest of it sound like a lie.

"What about Robbie?" I asked him. "What happened to her?"

He shook his head. "I don't know. She left with Bob on Wednesday afternoon, as I told you. And I haven't seen her since then."

I studied his face and said, "I don't think I believe you, Mr. Clinger."

"I didn't expect you to," he said. "Your job is to be suspicious. Nevertheless, I'm telling you the truth. She was with us for a time, and then she left."

"As simple as that," I said.

"Robbie was a free agent, just as we all are."

"She was also fourteen."

"And what of it," he said a bit angrily. "What does her age have to do with her capacity to enjoy life in her own way. Or do you believe that happiness has a date on it? Do you think she should have kept on leading a life that was a living hell because the law said that she was too young to know her own mind?"

It was a reasonable question and there was only one way of answering it. "How happy is she now?"

"That's beside the point," he said bitterly. "She chose to leave with a boy who loved her. And I am not responsible for that or for the accidents of fate."

"Then exactly what are you responsible for?" I asked him.

"For myself," he said. "And only myself."

But it wasn't that simple, and Clinger was smart

enough to know it. I could tell from the defensive tone of voice and the angry look on his face that he wasn't comfortable or satisfied with his own explanation.

"Our talk is finished," he said and got up off the piano bench. "Your car is parked outside. Get in it and drive away from here."

"Just like that?" I said with a laugh. "It won't be that easy, Theo. I know about the drug deals. I know about the kind of men you've been doing business with. And I'm going to go to the police with what I know."

"You do what you have to do," he said. "I have nothing to fear from the police."

He sounded so confident that it bothered me.

"I wouldn't count on Irene Croft's help, Theo," I said to him. "She's pulling out on you. Her family is making her pull out."

"Irene is a loyal friend," he said. "But she is a free agent, too. I have no need of her help. I'm not guilty of any crime."

I could have told him what he was guilty of, but I didn't think he would have understood me.

I got up off the couch and my leg almost collapsed beneath me. The ankle was stiff from the fall and I had to nurse it along, hobbling down a hallway to the front door and out onto the porch.

It was early morning—the sun just rising over the hedge of lilacs. The farm yard was deserted, except for the Pinto, parked beneath the apple tree. I glanced back through the door, into the dark house. Upstairs a girl laughed easily and a man sighed. Clinger's family, I thought. His sleepy children, for whom he bore no responsibility. The doctrinaire son-of-a-bitch.

I looked back at the yard and knew that out there in

196

the morning twilight, in a weed field or a backwater, Robbie Segal might be sleeping, too. The victim of . . . I didn't know what to call it. Of the red, lubricious thread of selfishness that ran from that porch across the river to the high towers of Mt. Adams and then over the green hills to Eastlawn Drive. The victim of the violence that sprang up like a spark whenever love turned doctrinaire and self-regarding. And yet she had been truly loved. Bobby Caldwell had loved her. And it hadn't been enough.

I worked my way down the steps into the yard. Clinger came out on the porch and watched me hobble over to the car. My ankle was killing me, and my head was spinning, but I'd be damned if I was going to let him know it.

"I'll be back, Theo," I called out as I got into the Pinto. "You can count on it."

"No, you won't, Mr. Stoner," he called back. "You're not welcome here any more. If you value your life, you'll stay away."

I managed to drive myself to Clifton, although I had to stop a few times to let my head clear. It was a bad concussion—the kind that could leave me with ringing ears and nervous tics and double vision. But the only treatment was bed rest, and I simply didn't have the time to spare.

When I got to the Delores, I washed my head off in the bathroom sink, bandaged my temple with gauze, taped my ankle, took three aspirins, and went to bed. I set the alarm for noon, which gave me five hours to recuperate. As I was drifting off, I thought of what Clinger had said about a friend of mine telling him who I was. I figured that that friend had to be Grace. I didn't really know anyone else who stayed at the farm—at least, anyone else who qualified as a friend. If it *had* been Grace, she'd probably saved my life, because, in spite of his cool, candid manner of speaking, Clinger was a desperate man. Only a desperate man would hire dumb, trigger-happy muscle like Logan to protect him.

Clinger was the last thing I thought of before I fell asleep. But I dreamed of Robbie and Bobby Caldwell— a sad, violent dream that woke me up before the alarm had gone off.

I tried going back to bed, but my head hurt too badly. And I knew that there was too much left to do. So I got up, took a quick shower and three more aspirins, emptying the rest of the bottle in a coat pocket. As I dressed, I reconsidered Clinger's explanation of what had happened to Bobby and the lost girl—that they had been killed by his "enemies."

In as far as any tragedy can be adequately explained, it seemed a reasonable story. He'd gotten in over his head on a drug deal and his enemies had taken it out on his family. But the very fact that it had come from Clinger—a man I didn't trust or like—made me search out inconsistencies. And the closer I looked, the more of them I found. For one thing, the murder had been an amateur job; and while there were plenty of two-bit druggies wandering around, living on their own pills and macho fantasies, they didn't seem like the kind of men Clinger would have been trading with. He'd needed big money to refloat his empire, and the big money pushers —the ones who wore business suits—didn't leave bloody fingerprints all over their victims. Moreover the crime had not been done gangland style. It was too messy for that, too hateful, too full of joy in the boy's pain. Bobby had been killed by someone who'd wanted to watch him die, someone who'd enjoyed it. And that meant someone with a personal grudge. True, the grudge could have been against Clinger, as he himself had claimed. But if that were the case, he'd managed to provoke a hell of a lot of anger in someone who was an obvious psychopath. And that had been a very stupid and unbusinesslike thing for a man as shrewd as Clinger to do.

I suppose that the biggest inconsistency in Clinger's explanation of the murder was the behavior of the girl herself. On Sunday night, Robbie had practically thrown herself at any man in The Pentangle Club. On Monday, she'd astonished Annie by sleeping with half the men at the farm. On Tuesday, she'd had a violent argument with Bobby and Theo about whether or not she should leave Clinger's paradise. In the face of all that contrary evidence, I wondered why on Wednesday she had suddenly changed her mind and gone with Caldwell. It wasn't simply that the choice didn't jibe with the facts as I knew them, it didn't jibe with my intuitive feeling about the girl, either. I'd convinced myself that she'd been using Bobby to get away from Eastlawn Drive—that while she might have loved him, she hadn't been consumed by him, as he had been by her. Robbie had wanted something more than Bobby Caldwell—she'd wanted that delirious, unfettered sense of freedom that Clinger apostled and the farm represented. I now thought that that had been the true meaning of the drunken look of pleasure on her face in the second photograph. It hadn't been drugs *or* sex that had made her look so high, although they'd been part of it. It had been the pure thrill of escape. And her behavior at the bar and at the farm confirmed it. More than Bobby Caldwell, more than the security of a lover, she'd wanted out— away from her mother and her house and anything else that smacked of Eastlawn Drive.

Of course, I could have been wrong about the girl. She might have had her fling and decided to return home. But the decision seemed too precipitous—too out of character. And my doubts about her change of heart cast doubt on everything else Clinger had told me.

I walked into the living room and sat down at the rolltop desk. I had two calls to make—one to George DeVries at that D.A.'s office and one to Art Bannock. George was an expert on the narcotics traffic in the city —just the man to ask about big-time drug dealers and their clientele. And as for Bannock, I wanted to find out how much he knew about Bobby's death and about Clinger's "enemies."

24

I GOT THROUGH TO GEORGE DEVRIES IMMEDIATELY AND made an appointment to see him at one-thirty. I was about to call Bannock when someone knocked on the door. I put the receiver back in its cradle, walked over to the peephole, and took a look outside. Jerry Lavelle was standing in the hallway. I couldn't see much of him through the fish-eye lens—just the tanned head, the creased blue eyes, and the jewelry smiling on his chest. He was wearing another leisure suit—carmine red—and a brown, open-collared shirt.

I figured it was no coincidence that he'd come calling the morning after I'd been to Clinger's farm. Just to be on the safe side, I stepped back to the desk and took a revolver out of the drawer. I slipped it in my coat pocket before unlatching the lock.

"Hello, Harry," Lavelle said in his genial, Vegas greeter's voice. "Mind if I come in?"

He glanced at the bruises on my temple and made a sympathetic face. "Terrible. Just terrible."

"What is it you want, Lavelle?" I said.

"You going to make me stand out in the hall?"

I backed away from the door and he stepped in.

"I'm just here to talk business, Harry," he said, opening the flaps of his coat to show me he wasn't armed.

"What kind of business?"

He sat down on one arm of the sofa and took a stick of gum out of his pocket. He peeled off the foil and folded the gum into his mouth. "Things have changed since I talked to you last," he said, chewing noisily on the gum. "What a tsimmes! That Irene . . . she doesn't stay put. She doesn't do the smart thing. The family is very worried." He shook his bald head mournfully.

"You a family man, Harry?" he said suddenly.

Lavelle didn't wait for an answer. He dug furiously into his coat and pulled out a leather wallet. He flipped it open like a cigarette holder and handed it to me. "My wife and children," he said proudly.

I glanced at the snapshot. A bland-looking woman in a housecoat was standing on a porch. Two teenage kids were standing beside her.

"The family means everything to me," Lavelle said with great feeling. "Without them, I'd be dead today. Swear to God. I don't make a move without we talk it over first. A man's nothing without his family, Harry. He's like an orphan at a picnic. He hasn't got a thing to call his own."

If the situation hadn't been so ridiculously inappropriate, I might have found his pride touching. It reminded me of Fred Rostow's dream of family life. But then Jerry Lavelle probably lived on a nice suburban street in a modest, well-kept home. In the light of his own sentimental hopes, you could almost mistake him for an ordinary, middle-class businessman, with a wife and two kids and a thirty-year mortgage. Only I wasn't in a sentimental mood.

"What do you want, Lavelle?" I said and handed him the photograph.

"I want you to be reasonable," he said, tucking the wallet back in his coat. "I want you to keep an open mind and hear me out."

"I'm listening."

"Let me be honest with you," he began. "A few years ago, the Croft family hired a private detective—a man like you. A professional. They wanted him to keep an eye on Irene—to steer her away from trouble. So everything's fine up until a couple of months ago when the detective finds out Irene's gotten herself mixed up with this Clinger. A very bad business. Well, I guess I don't have to tell you." He nodded at my bandages and cracked his gum.

"Drugs," he said. "They're an abomination, Harry. Personally I never go near them—not even prescription. And let me tell you . . . if I ever found one of my children smoking pot, they'd live to regret it. If somebody'd taken the time to give Irene the right kind of instruction, the family wouldn't be in this mess. But what's the use of talking? The fact is she got herself involved with this bum, with this Clinger. And with the drugs and the sex. A young boy gets killed. A girl is missing. It's a very bad business. And now she's gone back over there—to that farm."

"She's back with Clinger?" I said.

Lavelle nodded. "This morning," he said, with a look of disgust. He slapped his hands on his knees. "What to do? The Crofts are all upset. And who could blame them? They're in the insurance business. Very big. If I took you down there and showed you their operation . . . I mean this is a hell of an organization, Harry. I'm talking millions. Nationwide. Been in business for better than a hundred years. Got a reputation like Lloyd's of London. They got life, auto, home, theft—all the lines. But you know what Mr. Croft himself said to me? He said, 'Jerry, nobody buys from us because they think they're going to save a dollar. They buy our name.' " He smiled as if it were a clever parable. "That's what they're selling, Harry. Their name. They're selling trust. 'Trust us. We know what's right for you. We got the experience.' You follow me?"

"I follow," I said. "The Crofts want me off the case."

Lavelle got a pained look on his pleasant face. "That's one way to put it," he said.

"Why?"

"I just told you why. They got a wacko woman on their hands they can't control. And they don't want her slinging crap on the rest of the family."

"And what about Bobby Caldwell?" I said.

Lavelle looked confused. "Who's that?"

"The boy who was murdered."

"Terrible," he said heavily. "A young boy like that. But let me ask you this . . . is slopping mud on the Crofts going to bring him back to life? As I understand it, the boy was killed by some doped-up drug peddlers. By scum. And I say they deserve everything they get. Let the police find them. It's their job. Let the police find out where the blame lies, and let justice be done."

I began to get a sick feeling in my gut. "The Crofts don't care if the cops investigate the boy's murder?"

"Why should they care?" Lavelle said with a shrug.

I sighed. "You bought the police off, too, didn't you, Jerry?"

Lavelle looked deeply offended. "We don't buy off anybody. This is America. We're businessmen. The

204

Crofts don't expect to get something for nothing. Now with this boy, this Bobby Caldwell, some arrangements can be made. A suitable annuity can be paid to his family. We aren't heartless animals. We got a *quid pro quo* for you, too."

"I can hardly wait."

Lavelle grinned like a horse trader. "We got the girl, Harry."

I stared at him for a moment. "You mean Robbie?" I said with astonishment.

"Who else?"

"Then she's alive?" I said.

Lavelle smiled broadly. "Absolutely. She's at the farm right now."

"That's not what Clinger told me."

"He was nervous," Lavelle explained. "He was worried about her. She had a rough time at home. He didn't want to send her back."

"And what makes you think you can get him to hand her over to me?"

"Hey, Clinger's a businessman, too," Lavelle said, and I knew he was right. "He'll see the light. It may take a couple of days. We need to straighten a few things out for him. Get a little heat off his back. But it'll all work out. In two, three days she'll be back with her family."

For a moment, I really didn't know what to say. I'd begun to think she was dead—murdered by accident or for some reason I hadn't yet discovered—and suddenly she was being handed back to me, out of the grave, by this genial hoodlum with the businesslike manners.

"Why can't I get her right away? Why the delay?"

"These things take time, Harry," he said. "Use your

205

head. Clinger's still afraid he's going to get gunned down on his front porch."

It did make sense. All I could think to say was, "I'll have to discuss it with her mother."

Lavelle held up a hand. "Take your time. Spend the day. I'll be back in touch tomorrow."

He got off the couch and walked back to the door. "What a world," he said sadly. "A boy is killed. A family is almost ruined." He shook his head and left, closing the door gently behind him.

It took me a couple of minutes to get my bearings after Lavelle had gone. I'd been hit on the head once that morning; and the news that Robbie was alive hit me like a second blow. I sat down, stunned, in the desk chair and stared blankly at the phone. I knew that I should probably call Mildred right away. I knew that she was sitting by the phone at that very moment, waiting for the call. Finding out that Robbie was all right would probably send her straight into shock. She'd break down and cry it all out—all the anguish and the guilts. Then she'd sleep around the clock. When she awoke, she could begin to take accounts again—to make provisions in her patient and proper way for the return of her daughter.

I stared at the phone and knew that I should make the call. And yet I held back. It wasn't that I hadn't believed Lavelle. What he'd proposed seemed straightforward. I'd swap Irene Croft for the girl, allowing the Crofts a couple of days to buy off Theo and his enemies. Old man Caldwell would get his annuity. Irene and Theo would come away unscathed. And Mildred would get Robbie back. It was as neat and efficient as an insurance policy, an actuary's idea of a fairytale ending. I think I was a little awed at the ease with which the Crofts—those folks who knew best, who set the standards around this town —had signed everyone up. Me, Theo, Robbie, Pastor Caldwell. Bannock, too, if I'd read Lavelle correctly. There was even a possibility that the terms of their insurance policy actually reflected the truth. Clinger had claimed the Caldwell boy had been killed by his enemies. Of course, he'd lied about Robbie, but there was little reason to believe that Bobby's death hadn't been a revenge killing. And if the killers turned out to be small-time druggies, my reservations about the circumstances of the murder could be removed. It was a nifty deal, all right. And the only thing holding me back—keeping me from picking up the phone and calling Mildred—was the sure knowledge that neither Lavelle nor the Crofts nor Clinger had been telling me the whole truth.

I could believe that the Croft family had a pathological fear of scandal. I could even believe that business might suffer, locally, from a criminal proceeding against Irene. What I couldn't quite believe was that they would engage in a widespread criminal conspiracy, a true obstruction of justice, just to keep Irene from being fingered as a drug peddler. They simply didn't have to go to that much trouble to keep her out of jail. A smart lawyer, a friendly judge, the right witnesses, a little tampering with evidence, and she wouldn't even be indicted. In fact, there wasn't any evidence, except for the dead boy.

Of course, the Crofts were a prudent family, used to taking extreme precautions. And perhaps that was why the conspiracy seemed too elaborate for the crime. But I didn't really believe that. What I believed was that there had been a brutal murder committed at or near the farm, and that Lavelle and the Crofts were more

207

than a little afraid that Irene or her friend Theo or some-one else at the farm had been criminally responsible. That suspicion made sense of their proposals, because what they were doing, in essence, was making the farm and the people on it disappear. If Clinger's empire didn't exist, then nothing scandalous or criminal could have taken place within its confines. No drug deals and no murders.

Of course no one would really be hurt by the scam. Clinger could always refloat his kingdom at a later date. Irene could move back to her lonely castle and brew up more trouble for the Crofts. Robbie would return home —at least for the night. And the only casualty—outside of the hopes of a handful of kids like Annie—would be Bobby Caldwell, who was beyond feeling disappointment or pain. He was the only real sacrifice, and even his death could be sweetened up with money. And if I knew Pastor C. Caldwell, he'd jump at the Crofts' deal.

But as I sat there by the phone, I knew that I wasn't satisfied with the arrangement, with the deliberate sacrifice of a love-struck teenager. He'd swallowed the crap that Clinger had preached about love. He'd preached it himself to Robbie and watched it sour into something amoral and strange—something as tainted as the farm itself. And yet he hadn't given up hope. He'd remained loyal to the girl up to the end. The world owed him something for that—some manner of justice—because he'd been better than the world had expected or wanted him to be. And that made him indismissible. I decided to hold off on the Croft deal and the call to Mildred until I'd found out exactly what had happened to the boy.

25

ONCE I GOT OUT IN THE REAL WORLD, FULL OF THE glare of April sunlight, my righteous indignation waned and I started to realize just how much that beating had taken out of me. I hobbled to the parking lot, head bent, eyes on the pavement. And by the time I got to the car, I'd broken into a light sweat. Young Galahad could scarcely hold onto the hard plastic steering wheel or guide his car out into traffic. He was a goddamn menace on the roads, weaving down Reading, through the spacious, sunlit overpasses of the expressways, to the northeast edge of town.

On my left, Mt. Adams rose up into the blue afternoon sky, a woody hillside laced with spring green. I squinted at it with regret. Just the thought of having to climb to the top of it—to that monied plateau overlooking the river—and to search out Grace wearied me, and Saturday had only begun.

I managed to make it to the Court House Building— a huge stone temple on the east side of town—and to park in the square. But it took me another few minutes to actually step out into the street. I swallowed a couple more aspirins dry and bulled my way through the crowd of lawyers and crooks, up the hundred concrete stairs to the dark lobby of the Court House. I rested against a pillar, while passersby gaped at my bandaged head and bruised face. My ankle smarted from the climb, but I could live with the pain. It was the dizziness and the nausea that wracked me. I figured if I could survive the next few hours they would subside, because a lot of the sick feeling was just bone weariness. I hadn't gotten enough sleep, and my whole body felt out of focus. I bought a cup of coffee from a vending machine, choked it down, then tackled the brass stairway that led up to George DeVries's office. I still wanted to confirm Clinger's drug connection—just to make sure that Logan and his buddy had been hired to ward off Clinger's enemies and not to sap nosy detectives looking into a murder.

I stumbled down the broad hallway, past the varnished oak doors of court rooms and judges' chambers. And at the end of the corridor, I got to the D.A.'s offices.

A secretary was sitting at a desk in front of George's room. I startled her with my beaten face.

"My God," she said in a flat, midwestern voice. "What happened to you?"

She was a middle-aged brunette with the bleary, sagging features of a heavy drinker. I stared at her a moment and said, "You don't want to know."

She nodded as if she agreed with me and pressed a button on the intercom. "Mr. DeVries?"

George came out of the office and said, "What is it, Helen?" Then he noticed me standing there and his puckered, brick red face turned assessorial—a look like a long, drawn-out whistle.

"Jee-*zus!*" he said between his teeth. "What happened to you?"

210

"That's what I wanted to talk to you about, George."

"Well, come right in, Harry." He waved his arm and stepped away from the door.

"Jee-zus," he said again when he'd sat down behind his desk. He shook his head and laughed nervously. "You're a sight."

I didn't think it was particularly funny and told him so.

"No offense, Harry," he said wryly. "I just didn't think there were many men who could take you like that."

"There aren't," I snapped. And then felt foolish for having said it. I had nothing to prove to George DeVries, although for one naked moment it hadn't felt that way. That moment passed and I found myself sitting across from a run-down cop with the craggy face of a red-headed Carl Sandburg. He wasn't a very smart cop, but he was ruthless and efficient—a tough man who probably thought he'd earned the right to pass judgment on me.

He sat back in his chair, tented his fingers at his lips, and said, "You need some help, Harry?"

I knew the kind of help he meant, and I resented the offer. "I can still take care of myself, George. What I need is some information."

"What about?" he said.

"A man named Theo Clinger."

He made a puzzled face to indicate that the name rang no bells. So I explained the drug deal to him, leaving out any mention of the Caldwell boy or of the missing girl.

"What I really want to know," I said when I'd finished, "is whether any drug dealers have put out a contract on him. Or if anyone had a big enough grudge to have wanted to give him grief."

"What kind of grief?" DeVries said.

"Murder."

He smiled as if I'd named one of his kids. "You know

211

there are an awful lot of people in this city dealing drugs, Harry. And every damn one of them is dangerous if he's pushed hard enough."

"I realize that, George. But let's narrow it down to heroin or cocaine dealers. And from what I know about Clinger, the deal that fell through was probably a large one."

"That's a much smaller ballpark," DeVries admitted. "You have any idea why the deal fell apart?"

"I think that one of his backers dropped out at the last moment, leaving Clinger holding the bag."

DeVries scraped his chin with a dirty thumbnail. "That could do it, all right. Those boys tend to get mighty anxious where money is concerned, especially if they'd fronted some of the stuff".

"That's what I figured."

"I'll see what I can do," he said, leaning back in his chair. "And give you a call tonight."

After finishing with George, I dragged myself back down to a phone booth in the lobby and rang up Central Station. I wanted to talk to Al Foster, who was the closest thing to a friend I had on the force. But he wasn't at his desk. I told the duty sergeant to tell him I'd drop around in a half an hour, hung up, and walked out into the day.

I spotted a little storefront bar and grill across the square and gazed at it longingly. I knew that liquor was the last thing I needed with a concussion. I also knew that it was the first thing I needed if I was going to stay on my feet. I tossed a mental coin; when it came up tails, I tossed it again and walked across Elm to the bar.

The bartender—a chunky Irishman with a shock of red hair and a square, pit-marked face—didn't look terribly impressed with my wounds. But in a Court House bar, he probably saw his share of bruises and bandages daily. I ordered a Scotch and another. And by the time I put the three dollars on the bar, I was feeling moderately improved. I knew that I'd probably pay for those drinks again, later in the day, when the buzz wore off. But there was always more Scotch, I thought cheerfully. Like death and taxes, it could be depended on.

I almost enjoyed the drive over to Ezzard Charles. The pain in my head was still there, but it had withdrawn a pace or two into the distance. And the nausea had gone away completely. Even my ankle felt better, as I stepped out of the car and walked to the Police Building.

I sailed past the desk sergeant and up to the second floor—to Al Foster's tiny office. I didn't even bother to knock.

He was bent over his desk when I walked in. All I could see of him was his shiny bald spot and the smoky white line of the cigarette in his mouth. When he looked up and saw me standing there, his long rubbery face went slack and the cigarette drooped between his lips like a tongue depressor.

"You're getting too old for this business, Harry," he said in his high-pitched, sardonic voice.

I sat down on a corner of his desk and said, "You may be right."

"Who did it?"

"A boy by the name of Logan."

He nodded listlessly. "And next time, his name will be Smith or Jones."

"You worried about me, Al?"

"Have you taken a good look at yourself in a mirror lately?"

"There was one in a bar in Elm Street," I said. "I stared into it for a while."

"I'll bet," he said drily. He made a little pile of the stuff on his desk, then slapped his hands on top of it like a paperweight. "You push too hard, Harry. You always have. Sometimes it's smarter to let up."

He was usually the most impersonal of men, and the sudden solicitude surprised me. Maybe it was the booze, but I found myself getting angry. "I'll take care of my house," I said coldly. "You take care of yours."

"And what does that mean?"

"It means you've got a cop in homicide who may be taking his orders from outside the department."

Whether it was true or not—and I was hoping Al could tell me—he hadn't liked to hear me say it. That was police business, and I was an outsider. He took a deep breath and said, "Take it up with the public prosecutor. I don't want to hear about it."

"It's important, Al," I said.

"Yeah, it's always important when a cop's involved."

"Will you give me a chance to explain?"

He tamped the cigarette out in a tin ashtray and shook a fresh one from a crumpled pack. His eyes had gone cold and vague, as if he'd stopped caring about what was said. I went ahead and told him anyway. Because I was a little drunk and a little angry and because whether he wanted to hear it or not, I wanted to say it. I told him everything about the case, from the Segal girl's disappearance through Lavelle's visit. And then I told him what I suspected.

"Bannock's in the Croft family's pocket, Al. I don't know how firmly, but he's in there. And if he can make

214

the case without involving Irene Croft, he's going to do it."

"And why not?" he said. "There's no proof that she and Clinger are involved in the Caldwell boy's murder."

"Maybe not. But they could be involved and we'd never know it, because the Crofts don't want the question to come up."

He took a drag off the Tareyton and squinted at me through the smoke. "Take it up with Bannock," he finally said.

"I'm taking it up with you, Al."

"And I told you I don't want to hear it," he snapped. "Bannock knows his business."

"Yeah, he's a credit to the force."

"You son-of-a-bitch," Foster said. "You don't even have a case, and you've got him convicted."

"That's why I'm talking to you, Al, instead of to a grand jury."

He scowled at his desk.

I said, "All I'm asking you is whether it's possible—whether Bannock could be a crooked cop."

"Anything's possible," he said coldly.

"Will you look into it?" I asked him. "Just nose around. See if he's connected?"

"I'll think about it," Foster said.

26

I WASN'T SURE THAT FOSTER WOULD FOLLOW UP ON what I'd asked him to do. But then I'd asked him to do what, in his book, was a dirty thing—to impugn the integrity of a brother officer. The fact that Bannock might actually be implicated in a conspiracy to obstruct justice was beside the point. No cop likes to fink on another cop —it was really that simple.

As I walked downstairs and out to the car, I decided not to count on Foster's help. Which left me feeling very much alone. My only hope was finding Grace and getting her to talk to me about the Caldwell boy's murder. She wouldn't make much of a witness in her high heels and feathered hats, but I didn't really need a witness—just the threat of one. It had occurred to me, as I was talking to Foster, that the Croft family was peculiarly vulnerable to threats. It was the threat of scandal that had started the whole conspiracy. And that morbid fear of scandal could be turned against them, if I could manage to convince Lavelle that it would be smarter to let the truth come out than to go ahead with the cover-up. And to convince him of that I needed to know precisely what had happened on Wednesday afternoon. I needed to know at least as much as the Crofts did about the boy's death.

Of course, my plan was predicated on the assumption that there *was* something to cover up—that Bobby Caldwell had not died at the hands of some hophead with a very bad temper. And the only way to confirm that assumption was to talk to someone who knew the truth.

I stood beside the Pinto and gazed up over the domed roof of Music Hall at the green fringe of hillside on the eastern horizon. It was time to make that climb again, I thought. To the top of Mt. Adams, where I hoped Grace would be waiting with what I needed to know.

That Saturday afternoon, Mt. Adams seemed filled with a sleepy beauty. The cobbled streets, the colorful houses had the dazed, sun-suffused look of a town in the tropics. White walls and dark spaces. All life gone torpid and weary. I coasted down Hill Street, past Corky's—its doors wide open, the bar just a woody gleam amid the dark, empty tangle of chairs and tables. Below me, the Ohio made a muddy, glistening path between the steep green hills on either bank. The river had the imposing look of a borderline that afternoon—something to be crossed over. But then I was thinking ahead to the ferry and the farm.

I dropped down to the Celestial Street plateau and parked beneath a hackthorn on the south side of the street. Up the block, the black roof of The Pentangle Club twinkled in the sun.

My head had begun to feel heavy again and I had to blink to focus my eyes. It was the concussion, coming back to life. I wanted another drink. I wanted to go to sleep, like that sunny hillside. To curl up and forget Bobby Caldwell and Robbie Segal and Grace. But I made myself walk the length of the block, past the wrought-iron fences and the blank wooden facades of the tired houses, up to the long porch. I stopped for a moment on the bottom step, wondering if she would be inside, as Joey had said she would be on a Saturday afternoon, or if she had bolted like Annie when she'd realized how dangerous a place Clinger's farm had become. I actually held my breath as I mounted the stairs and stepped through the door. And let it back out—in a long, grateful sigh—when I found her sitting on the stool, humming a melancholy tune.

"Grace?" I said softly. She stopped singing and looked up.

Her pale face filled with pain when she saw me. Her eyes touched at the bandages on my head and the purple bruises on my cheek, and she brought her hand to her own temple and held it there, like a sympathetic salute.

"My God. My God, your head."

"If it wasn't for you, it would have been much worse," I said and felt a rush of gratitude to her that made me blush. I looked away—partly because I was embarrassed and partly because I needed her help again and didn't know how to ask for it.

She lowered her hand and touched delicately at my cheek. Her fingers felt like snow.

"I didn't really see—last night. I didn't know how badly they'd hurt you. Those sons-of-bitches," she said furiously and her eyes slid from my face to the floor. "I'm sorry."

"You don't need to apologize," I told her. "You saved my life. They would have killed me."

218

She looked up and started to say something—something, perhaps, in explanation. But when she saw my bruises again, she merely nodded.

There was no subtle way to ask, so I came right out with it. "I need your help again, Grace. I need some information."

She shook her head. "I can't. They know I know you, now. And they don't like it. I just can't, Harry."

"If you can't, then who can?" I said to her. "If you can't, then Bobby Caldwell might as well not have lived."

"I'm telling you they'll kill me, Harry," she said desperately. "I'm sorry for Bobby, but I have to think of myself."

I studied her for a moment and couldn't bring myself to threaten her or cajole her—not after what she'd done for me. "All right," I said heavily. "I'll find some other way."

I turned to leave. I was through the door when I heard her whisper, "Wait."

I looked back.

"You just can't leave her there," Grace said with a kind of exhausted compassion.

"Do you mean Robbie?"

She nodded. "I heard them talking this morning. Irene and Logan. You can't leave her there. Theo's all she's got, and he's weak." She said it bitterly.

"You want to go somewhere and talk about it?"

She looked over at Joey, who was rinsing glasses and stacking them on the bar. "I guess we better," she said. "But you've got to help me, man. You've got to get me out of this city."

"I'll get you out," I promised her.

"To L.A.," she said.

"All right. To L.A."

"Then take me to that funky apartment of yours and let's talk."

As we walked out of the bar into the waning sunlight, I couldn't help asking her, "Why did you change your mind?"

She looked straight ahead—at the sleepy, unpeopled street. "Why did I help you last night?" she said in a bemused voice. "Good Karma, I guess. Good for the music."

And very good for me, I thought. And for Robbie, too.

When we got back to the Delores, Grace walked directly to the bedroom and sat down on the edge of the mattress. She looked considerably less resolute than she had when we'd struck the deal in Mt. Adams. But then she had good reason to be afraid. If the Crofts found out about her, she might end up as another *quid pro quo* in Jerry Lavelle's insurance policy. That was why I couldn't use her as a witness. No matter what she told me, I was going to leave her out of it. It was the only certain way to keep her safe.

I walked back to the bedroom and sat down beside her on the bed. She glanced at me nervously.

"You don't think anybody saw us, do you?" she said.

It was a thought that had bothered me—that Lavelle might have been having me watched. But I hadn't seen anyone hanging around the lot or the building, and I was fairly certain we hadn't been followed home.

I told her no, but her eyes stayed frightened.

"I want you to do something for me, O.K.?" she said and didn't give me a chance to reply. "I know you're in

220

bad shape, but I want you to hold me. I mean, you don't have to fuck me. Just hold me for awhile."

I put my arms around her and she curled up beside me. Together we watched the sunlight dying in the bedroom window.

"You feel like talking?" I said to her after a time.

I felt her nod. "I guess so."

"You said something before about Robbie needing help. What did you mean?"

Grace pulled the blanket over her legs and lay her head on my thigh. "I heard them talking," she said. "This morning. In the kitchen. I think Logan and Irene want to get rid of her."

"You mean kill her?"

Grace nodded.

"Why?"

"She knows," Grace said. "She knows about what happened to Bobby. She went off with him on Wednesday afternoon, and when she came back, she was hysterical. I think she would have killed herself if Theo hadn't been there. He's been looking after her ever since."

I took a breath and said, "What did happen to Bobby?"

"I don't know it all," she said.

"Then tell me what you do know."

She hugged herself tightly under the blanket and closed her eyes. "Bobby came to the farm on Wednesday afternoon. He'd been there every day since Sunday, when he dropped Robbie off. She'd been acting like a whore all week, sleeping with everyone. She even slept with Irene, and you had to be crazy to do that. Irene really dug it, too. I think that's what was bothering Bobby the most—that Irene was screwing Robbie. And I mean all the time. The girl just walked around with this

221

sort of spaced-out look on her face, like she'd wandered into a candy store and there was nobody at the register, and every time Irene or one of the guys whistled, her eyes would go kind of hard and knowing. It was weird, like she only came alive when she was being screwed. And even then, it wasn't as if she understood what it meant. It was more of an animal thing. You could hear her screaming dirty words all over the house. At first, it was funny. Then it got old. And then it got kind of scary —especially when she was with Irene. It didn't sound like love-making. I don't know what it sounded like— something dirty and sick and cruel. It really got to me. And to Bobby worst of all. Man, he'd sit outside on the porch and you could just see his face crack up. I don't know how he could stand it."

"He loved her," I said softly.

"He really did," she said. "I guess he thought she'd get it out of her system. But I knew better. What's wrong with Robbie is part of her system. She was born with it. I even tried to talk to him about it. I told him to forget her. And he got furious and said I didn't understand her —that she'd had a hard time. I understood her, all right. Every one of us at the farm came from one screwed-up family or another. We were all outcasts and orphans. That was the beautiful thing about Theo. He gave us more than a place to stay—he gave us the home we never had. And it really was a family out there. Or it was until Irene came along."

"When was that?"

"About six months ago," she said. "Theo was having a bad time financially, so he told us he was going to make a sacrifice for the good of the family and take on a business partner. After that, Irene started coming out to the farm.

222

At first it was cool. She was really devoted to Theo, following him around like a puppy. It was like this was all some kind of new life for her—a new beginning. Theo dug it, too. He was always kind of vain, and she knew how to play on his vanity for all it was worth. Pretty soon, things began to change. Irene started bringing some of her weird-ass friends out to the farm. Converts, she called them, as if Theo were a kind of god or a religion. They began to party with us. Real wild affairs, with blow and smack. When you get that cooked, you stop thinking about what you're doing and just go with the flow. And that's pretty much what all of us did. It got to be an ugly scene. All the music drained away, and it was just dope and sex and Irene, sitting there in her black leather pants. Theo knew it was getting out of hand. He even threatened to kick her out if she didn't shape up. And for a while she acted meek and repentant. Then something happened a couple of weeks ago, and everything went to hell."

"Some men came to the farm," I said. "They threatened to kill Clinger."

Grace looked surprised. "How did you know that?"

"A girl named Annie told me."

"Annie!" Grace said. "Where is Annie?"

"In Denver, I think. That's where she said she was going."

"Annie," she said again.

"She told me that Clinger had gotten himself involved in a drug deal and that it hadn't worked out."

Grace nodded. "That's right. Irene was the one who talked Theo into the deal. She'd been feeding him money right along, but Theo had big debts. They figured one large deal might get him back on his feet again. She was going to finance it."

223

"What went wrong?" I asked her.

"Irene backed out at the last moment," she said. "She claimed she couldn't get the money together, but I think that was bullshit. I think she did it to show Theo who was really boss. And it worked, too. Because after that she practically moved out to the farm. And Theo didn't say a word. It seemed like their positions had completely reversed—like it was her place instead of his. She hired Logan and another man named Reese for protection. And the place started to look like an Army camp. That's when a lot of the family started to leave. That was the week that Robbie came."

"What happened on Wednesday?" I said.

"Bobby blew up. He came out to the farm and told Irene and Logan to keep their hands off Robbie. There was a fight and Theo had to step in to stop it. I think Logan and Reese would have killed Bobby if he hadn't stopped them. Robbie was crying and Theo was practically crying and Bobby was a mess. Theo really loved him, because he was so good-natured and talented. And Bobby loved Theo, too. He modeled himself after him. That was what made the scene so terrible. They were both crying and Bobby said that if Theo didn't let Robbie come with him, he was going to the cops and tell them about the drug deal. But Theo hadn't been keeping Robbie at the farm. She'd wanted to stay there. And Theo respected that. I don't know if Bobby was serious or not about the cops. I think mostly he just wanted Robbie back. She was all he ever really wanted."

"And Theo let her go with him?"

"She decided to go herself."

"Why?" I said.

"I don't know. She was pretty scared."

"Do you think she loved him?" I said—mostly to myself.

Grace thought about it for a second. "I think she wanted to," she finally said.

I got off the bed and walked over to the window. The sun was almost down. It hung above the elm trees in the back yard like a spot of blood in the sky. I stared into it and said, "Who killed Bobby Caldwell?"

"Irene," Grace said.

"How do you know?"

"I just think she did. She and Logan and Reese."

I turned back to the room and said, "I think she did, too."

27

NEITHER OF US SAID ANYTHING TO EACH OTHER FOR A time. I stared out the window, at the elms turning colors in the sunset, and Grace curled up again beneath the blanket. After awhile, I sat down beside her.

"You don't hate me, do you?" she said in a small unhappy voice.

"For what?"

"For being part of it? For not telling you about it the other day? I was thinking . . . maybe you wouldn't have gotten beaten up, if I hadn't lied to you before."

"No," I said. "I don't hate you."

Only I was thinking about Irene Croft, who'd told me that everyone lied. I was thinking that, in a world of liars, she'd finally come to the end of her patience and gone furiously mad. The violence must have been there all along, burning inside her—the home fires, the hearth. But she'd kept it banked for years, living off the contempt she felt for all those lies that other people told each other. Those lies had shaped the truth for her into something wicked and perverse. And somewhere in the last years or months that had led to Wednesday night,

226

somewhere between the drugs and the liaisons and the cold mornings after, that truth had driven her crazy. Perhaps the murder had seemed like an unselfish act to her—to kill the boy who threatened her beloved Theo. Or perhaps she'd ceased to care about Theo when his lies and his world had been exposed for the illusions that they were. Perhaps she'd ceased to care about anything but the red, appetitive fury inside her. That fury was the real meaning of the murder. And I knew that it was still burning and that, having broken out once, it would take even less provocation for it to break out again. She was already planning a second killing, in the face of her family's effort to hide the first one. Maybe that was why she was doing it—to throw their pride right back at them, soaked in Robbie Segal's blood. I wondered if Lavelle had known that that was what she'd been planning, if that was why he'd proposed to trade Robbie for my silence about the drugs and the Caldwell killing. Maybe it was the Crofts' way of saving the girl's life. Because they couldn't cover up a second killing—I simply knew too much and so did Grace and Theo and Bannock. Only Lavelle had needed a couple of days to set the conspiracy up—to pay off Clinger's debts and enlist Bannock and talk to Pastor Caldwell. What he didn't know was that those two days were going to be too long. That all that was standing between Robbie and a terrible death was one weak, vain man, who was hanging onto her as the last remnant of his own hopes. A little piece of hell was blazing in Clinger's farmyard, spewing terror like smoke and turning all the man's dreams and love into char. He wouldn't be able to hold out much longer, and if he did, perhaps Logan and Reese and the Croft woman would kill him, too.

227

Grace fell asleep in my arms, exhausted by her fears and memories. And I sat there beside her and wondered what I was going to do—without police help, without enough evidence to get the FBI interested, with certain violence waiting for me at the end of that dusty farm road. I wondered if the girl was even worth saving. Because she was as mad as the world she'd run off to—my lost Robbie. And that, in the end, had been the real difference between her and Eastlawn Drive. Not my romantic projections about freedom and conformity. Those had belonged to me, to the part of me that had been prodded to life by the dismal look of that street and the pitiless pieties of its householders. As Grace had said, her mother and the Rostows and all the rest of that gray neighborhood might have played a role in distorting the girl's character, but what was wrong with her couldn't finally be accounted for in terms of a house or a street or a neurotic mother. If I'd been smarter, less set on living out my own adolescent gripes, I could have seen it from the start. In the gape-mouthed stupor of her photograph. In all the broken plates and dishes that Mildred had pasted so patiently back together. In the hostile vagueness of the friends who had described her. In the mad scenes in the Pentangle bar and later at the farm. Saving her now—to be brought back to the cage of Eastlawn Drive—seemed pointless and cruel. How could she go back, I asked myself, after Irene and Bobby?

And in spite of the fact that I couldn't answer the question, in spite of the tragedy that would certainly ensue, I knew that I was going to go get her. Because no one else would. Not Bannock or Lavelle, who were perfecting their scheme of obstruction. Or Al Foster, who couldn't see beyond his badge. I couldn't even bring in the state cops, for fear that a bunch of police cars might send Irene into a final, murderous spasm. It had to be me. And the reason, finally, wasn't for her mother or for myself or for Robbie, either. It was for the boy who had loved her and died for her. If she hadn't meant a thing to anyone else, she meant the world to him. And that made her worth saving.

The bedroom had begun to go dark. The evening sky a violet skein drawn across the window, with just a thread or two of fire woven through it. I lifted Grace's head onto a pillow, got up, and walked into the living room. I sat down at the desk and took two envelopes out of the bottom drawer. I wrote Grace's name on one of them, got three hundred dollars in cash out of the cash box, and put the money in the envelope. I didn't seal it. Then I took a piece of paper from the desk and wrote down all I knew about the Robbie Segal case. When I finished, I stuck it in the second envelope.

I didn't know who to address it to. And finally settled on Al Foster. I thought of calling Mildred—to let her know what I was going to do. But the situation was so chancy—the girl's life so precariously balanced—that I decided she was better off not knowing that her daughter was still alive. Because in a matter of hours there was a very good chance that she wouldn't be—if I couldn't talk Clinger into giving her back or couldn't pry her away by force. It would have to be one way or the other. And I didn't have much faith in Theo, whose strength had been sapped by years of bad luck and by Irene Croft —who had become his nemesis.

I unlocked the gun drawer in the desk and took out the two pieces—a .45 Commander and a .357 magnum. I stuck the .45 in a belt holster and the .357 in a shoulder

229

holster and put them both on. Then I loaded five extra magazines with 230 grain hardball and stuck them in my pocket. I was wearing a good fifteen pounds of lead and brass and tempered steel, and I could feel it.

When I'd finished arming myself, I took a long look at my apartment—studying it like a detective. It wasn't much, I thought. A few books, a few unmatched pieces of furniture, a big table radio, a desk. The man who lived there didn't have much of a home. He didn't care much for things. He'd lived in the spaces between his belongings—in the shadows and the corners. In the teasing, empty places that his life had never filled.

I stood up. I wanted to say goodbye to someone, but the girl was still asleep and it seemed a shame to wake her. As I was stepping out the door, George DeVries called to tell me what I already knew—that Clinger had gotten himself in trouble over a drug deal.

It took me half an hour to get to the Anderson Ferry. I pulled off River Road and coasted down to the dock. It was another cold night. A westerly wind was chasing dark clouds across the sky. I got out and walked over to the bell post. The signal bell made the same cracked sound it had before. And in a minute, the answering bell echoed across the dark water. There was no fog on the river this night; and even in the cold I could smell the mud, washed into the long Ohio by the spring rains.

I stood on the dock, waiting for the ferryboat. And in a few minutes, I could see the faintly lit wheelhouse, emerging from the shadows of the Kentucky hills. The same boy was standing on deck, dressed in the same clothes. When he hopped off the boat onto the landing, I saluted him. But he didn't seem to remember me.

230

"Let's get going," he said. "We don't have all night."

I got into the Pinto and drove onto the barge. The deck rocked gently beneath me. I sat back in the seat and closed my eyes and listened to the sound of the winch and the puttering of the engine. The river slid past, tugging at the barge with its muddy fingers. I sat there for what seemed like many minutes, lulled and buoyed by the current. Then we docked with a bump, and the engine noises died away.

The boy stuck his head through the open window and said, "Two dollars."

I got the money out of my wallet. He took it from me and stared curiously into my face.

"Been in an accident?" he said.

"Headed for one," I told him and drove off the barge onto the landing and up the access road to the highway.

My headlights stabbed through the sycamore trees along the bank of the river, lighting up the same rusted refuse—the oil drums and tackle boxes and odd scraps of tire rubber. And then the trees died away, and the river came back into view, flowing placidly westward—the moonlight spread softly over it as if it had been spilled into the water. The highway turned inland, down that paltry avenue full of small, glassy motels and loaf-shaped metal diners. I passed Tillie's and her parking lot full of semis. And a mile or so farther on, the landscape flattened into featureless countryside—vacant acres of plowed fields and wind-bellied fencing. I drove through the dark, deserted flat land until my headlight caught on the sign posted on Clinger's gate.

I pulled off the highway and stopped. A chilly wind burned my face as I stepped out of the car. I stared at the sign—*Private Property*. And for the first time since I'd gotten in the car, I let myself think of what lay ahead of me—of what would happen if I couldn't talk Clinger into letting Robbie go or if Irene and Logan and Reese decided to stop me. There was violence ahead, burning undetected in the night.

I thought about Bobby Caldwell and Robbie. Thought that their disparate stories were coming to an end—that, like an author, I was adding my own life to theirs. And the story was love—nothing more. How it got lost behind that gatepost; how it got hidden in the mazy front yards of Eastlawn Drive; how it boiled away in a high, handsome Mt. Adams penthouse, where no one had thought to turn the fire off. That night, the world seemed full of love's failures. Men and women driven by a relentless, inexplicable urge to destroy the grounds of their own happiness—running from all charity and comfort, as if the charity itself was a burden and the comfort a baseless lie. And I counted myself among them. For lots of reasons. But mostly because I was standing in front of that gate, staring into the distant fire and preparing to stick my hand into the flames and pluck out what was left of Bobby Caldwell's heart.

I kicked the gate open and walked back to the car. I was going straight in this time. No stumbling through the dark in another man's preserve. There was the three of them and there was me. With Clinger standing somewhere in between. And the girl—she was lost in the night, waiting to be pulled out of the darkness, either to be saved or lost once again.

28

I FOLLOWED THE ROAD TO THE CREST OF THE HILL,
then stopped and looked down at the farmhouse. There
were lights burning in the kitchen and in one of the
upstairs windows. But there wasn't any movement behind the curtains or anywhere in the yard. There hadn't
been any movement the night before, either, when I'd
almost been killed. I touched at the bruise on my head
and felt a twinge of pain. Logan and Reese were tough
country boys. And they were more than a little crazy,
too, judging by what they'd let Irene talk them into
doing to Bobby. They liked dealing out pain, and they
wouldn't think twice about killing me, if they caught me
a second time. The thought sobered me.

I checked the .45 to make sure it was cocked and
locked. Took a deep breath of cold night air. And started
the engine again, heading down the gently sloping hill,
past the hedge of lilacs and the apple tree, into the deserted yard.

As I pulled up to the house, I caught sight of a man
sitting in the darkness of the porch overhang. I couldn't
tell who it was, but I wasn't going to take any chances.

I slipped the pistol out of the holster and held it by my side, as I stepped out of the car and walked up to the steps. It wasn't until I was standing directly in front of the porch that I realized that the man I'd seen was Clinger. He was sitting on a rocking chair in the darkness, staring out at his yard.

"Clinger?" I said.

But he didn't answer me. I started up the stairs. Then a wild, piercing laugh came out one of the upstairs windows, and I froze. Clinger didn't move.

I called his name again—softly. And when he still didn't move, I knew he wasn't going to answer me—or anyone else. I shuddered a little, walked up to the porch landing, and took a look at him. Not a long look. They'd tied him to the chair with chicken wire. One of his hands had been hacked off and the flesh of his cheeks had been sheared away, so that the back teeth were exposed on either side and his grin stretched from ear to ear. One of them had fashioned a crown out of brown paper and stuck it on his head, turning him into a grinning *memento mori*—the leering lord of his ruined kingdom.

There was a crash upstairs, followed by that demented laughter and more crashing noises. It sounded like they were tearing the place apart—breaking the house's bones, as they'd broken the bones of its master. I thought of what they might have done to the girl and was filled with a fury that had little to do with Caldwell or Clinger or Robbie herself. Hell was loose inside that farmhouse, and I hated it. I wanted to put an end to its reign. I unlocked the pistol and pushed at the front door. It opened noiselessly.

I stepped into the narrow hallway. There was a room

at the far end and two openings on the left wall. A staircase emptied into it midway down the right wall, and it was down that staircase that all the noise and laughter was coming. I slid down the left wall, peering into the two darkened rooms. In the faint light coming from upstairs, I could see that they'd both been savaged. Broken glass and china littered the floors; the Victorian furniture had all been gutted—stuffing dripped from every knifehole and slash mark. They'd even destroyed the piano in the parlor. The wires had been cut. They dangled from the sounding board like the legs of a centipede.

I skirted the staircase and peered into the room at the end of the hall—the kitchen. Every dish had been smashed. Food was spattered on the walls. The refrigerator lay on its side like a dead animal. I walked over to it and opened the door. Clinger's hand was lying inside on a vegetable rack. I kicked the door shut and turned back to the hall.

"Party's over!" I bellowed.

And the crashing sounds upstairs stopped.

"Come on down!" I shouted, and my voice sounded queerly inviting.

I walked over to the staircase and flattened myself against the wall on the left side of the opening.

"Boys and girls?" I called to them.

I could hear them talking upstairs. And then the house went quiet.

I took the magnum out of my belt with my right hand and cocked the hammer. I held it against my right side and, back against the wall, pointed the automatic in my left hand toward the staircase opening. Since I was pressed against the wall, all I could see of the stairway was the last step. But I could see either way down the hall—front and back.

There was a sound on the stairs and then a shotgun went off with a terrific bang. The buckshot tore a huge hole in the wall across from the staircase, filling the hallway with plaster dust and gunsmoke. Immediately after the gun went off, a naked man came charging down the stairs. He leaped into the hallway and looked to his left —toward the front door. A shotgun was poised in his hands. When he turned right and looked at me, I shot him. With both pistols.

The impact of the bullets sent him bouncing down the hall, spraying blood on either wall. He fell to the floor near the door, jerked crazily for a moment, and fired the shotgun into his own feet.

I stepped into the smoky stairway.

"I'm coming up!" I shouted.

I charged up to the first landing—the pistols in my hands. I flattened myself against the wall and pointed the guns at the top landing. A man darted from behind the left wall at the top of the stairs and fired a shotgun at me. I fired back as soon as I saw him. There was just a split second between our shots. The shotgun blast broke my left shoulder, and the .45 fell out of my hand. I tossed the magnum on the floor, picked up the Colt with my right hand, and climbed up to the landing. The one called Logan was lying in the hallway. The shotgun was still in his hand. There was a red, pulsing hole in his back. He turned his head and looked up at me. And I shot him again.

I was badly hurt, and I knew it. The buckshot had cracked some ribs and gone through into the left side of my chest. My shirt was soaked with blood and my left

236

arm was turned out at an odd angle. I bit my lips against the pain and wiped the blood from my mouth with my good hand.

"All right, Irene," I said, staring at a lighted room at the porch end of the hallway. "It's your turn, now."

A woman shrieked inside the lighted room. Then she came running out. She was naked, like the men. And her face was sheer madness. She fired a small caliber pistol at me as she ran. One of the bullets hit me in the right side, above the hip.

I groaned and returned fire with the automatic.

The bullet knocked her onto her back. She lay on the hall floor—panting.

I braced myself against the wall with my right hand and worked my way down the hallway to where she was lying. Her eyes were wide open. They darted from side to side, like the eyes of a dying animal. There was blood on her teeth and lips.

"Where is she?" I groaned. "Where's Robbie?"

The woman's fathomless black eyes just kept ticking back and forth, until they stopped, like the hands of an unwound clock.

I stepped around her body and into the room she'd come out of.

The place was a shambles, like everything else in that hellish house. But in a corner, bundled against the wall among the broken lamps and picture frames, was Robbie Segal. My Robbie. As mad and as naked as the other three. There were bloodstains on her fingers. From Clinger, I thought. She wiggled them at me and began to laugh.

For a moment, I felt like shooting her, too. Because it was clear now that she was as guilty as the rest of them.

"*You* killed him, didn't you, Robbie?" I said. "*You* killed Bobby Caldwell."

She laughed and laughed—her long blonde hair shaking on her shoulders. She wiggled her bloody fingers and laughed.

29

OF COURSE, THERE WAS NO WAY TO REALLY KNOW.

I thought later, in the hospital, that she might have gone with Bobby on impulse that Wednesday. Impulse seemed to be her only motivation. I thought that seeing him killed by the men and the woman she'd been sleeping with might have destroyed all that was left of her self-control. Grace had said that Robbie had been hysterical when she was brought back to the farm on Wednesday night. Grace had said that she'd tried to kill herself and that Theo had stopped her. But, of course, that didn't prove that she wasn't guilty of Bobby's murder or of taking a part in it. It was just as likely that she'd gone off with the Caldwell kid on Wednesday afternoon because Irene had told her to go—to lead him to his death, as he'd thought he was leading her to safety. Maybe Irene hadn't told her what she and Reese and Logan had planned for the boy. Maybe they'd left that for a surprise. They hadn't told her what they'd had planned for her, either—at the tail end of that bloody Saturday night. After the fun, after the devastation, it was my guess that they would have killed her, too, as Grace had heard them planning to do. And then, for all I knew, they might have turned on each other.

Maybe she'd loved him, I thought. Maybe she'd realized it on that fatal afternoon, when he'd stood up against all of them and braved death for her. But by Saturday night that love had been swallowed up in horror and in the madness that Irene Croft had spread like contagion, once she'd become the reigning queen of Clinger's blasted paradise.

The boy shouldn't have gone back for Robbie on Wednesday is what I finally thought. He should have listened to Grace and left her at the farm. But then he'd been the victim of his own sweet obsession and, in the end, he couldn't let her go. In the end, I couldn't either, although the girl I'd brought out of that charnel house might have been better off dead.

The case worked out strangely for all of us. Instead of being charged with murder, as I'd expected to be, I was visited one May afternoon, in the hospital where I was recuperating, by Jerry Lavelle and snowy-haired Arthur Bannock. Lavelle did most of the talking.

"Harry," he said, pulling a chair up to my bed. "How's the arm?"

The arm would never be the same—nor would the leg or the left lung—but I told him it was all right.

"That's fine. Just fine," he said cheerfully. "The cops talked to you, yet?"

"Every day," I said.

"Well, that'll probably stop," he said.

I stared at him uncertainly.

"A murder trial, Harry . . ." He shook his head and cracked his gum. "It's a terrible thing. One question leads to another and before you know it, you got a—"

"Scandal?" I supplied the word.

"Exactly," he said. "We don't want that, do we, Harry?
So we worked out a little deal for you. You cop a plea—
self-defense. And we'll see that it washes."

"And how will you do that?"

"Well, the four of them were loaded with drugs. The
coroner's report shows that. And they'd murdered the
Clinger man earlier in the evening. Their clothes were
covered with his blood. And the women had sperm in
them. So right away we got the sex angle, too. And the
rest is easy. You show up looking for Robbie. And high
on drugs and sex and bloodlust, they tried to murder
you."

"And what's the *quid pro quo?*" I asked him.

He smiled as if he loved the sound of the words. "The
Croft family never comes up. You don't know me or
Bannock or anything about our little deal."

"I can't prove anything about it, anyway," I said. "Why
the hell do you bother to cover it up?"

"You maybe can't prove anything," he said. "But a
friend of yours maybe can."

I thought about it for a moment and smiled. I glanced
over at Bannock, who was staring at me spitefully. "You
were born under a lucky star, boy-o," he said. "Make no
mistake about that."

I said, "It's Al Foster, isn't it? He looked into the case,
after all."

"He did more than look," Lavelle said woefully. "If we
can't work something out, he's going to blow this thing
sky high."

"I'll think about it," I told them, although there wasn't
much to think about. I wanted to expose the Crofts'

241

vicious conspiracy. But I also wanted to stay out of jail. And when it came down to it, self-interest won out.

Another week went by and I was released from the hospital.

I couldn't move around very well yet. It had practically been a miracle that the surgeons had managed to save my arm. It was still attached—with wire and plastic and metal rods. But it didn't move when I told it to. Nothing seemed to move right any longer. Not even my thoughts.

Something about the case—something beyond the savage bloodshed—had sapped my strength. I'd done my job. I'd gotten the girl back. But she'd been sent to an asylum, probably for the rest of her life. And I'd been left with nothing, except for bad dreams. I found myself thinking about leaving the city—putting some space between me and those dreams. I began to plan for it; it made the hours pass.

Spring spun on toward summer. The elm trees blossomed in the back yard. The dogwoods dropped their waxy pink petals on the sidewalks. And the nights began to smell of honeysuckle.

One Thursday toward the end of May, I drove out to see Mildred. We'd seen each other at the coroner's inquest. And again at Robbie's sanity hearing. But we hadn't spoken after that. So I decided to pay her a last visit—to say goodbye.

There was a blue Mayflower moving van parked in the driveway when I drove up Eastlawn to her tidy little house. I pulled up to the curb and watched the men in their green overalls carting out the furniture—the sofa with the floral print cover, the blue wing-back chairs,

242

paper boxes full of plates and glasses, the white rocker from Robbie's room. They stacked it all on the sunny lawn, then hoisted it onto the truck. It embarrassed me a little to see Mildred's life spread out in pieces for everyone to see.

I walked up the tar driveway to the front door. It was open.

I stepped inside and stared at the empty room. It looked small and naked without the furnishings. Mildred was standing in the dining room. She saw me and her long, horsey face went blank, as if I were just another stranger. I'd seen that look on her face during the hearing, as if she'd ceased to understand what the proceedings were about, as if they didn't connect with anything in her life. She'd blocked something off inside—some passageway to the heart—and had become a spectator at her daughter's trial. She hadn't even flinched when the court had sent Robbie to an institution. It was as if it were all happening to someone else, as if she'd disowned the experience. But then she was an economical woman and the cost of facing the truth—of feeling it fully—was simply too dear.

I didn't blame her for that. In my own way, I'd been doing the same thing. First, when I'd accepted Lavelle's offer. And second, when I'd begun to think of leaving. I, too, had stopped caring about what couldn't be helped. But then we were kin, she and I.

She said hello to me. And I asked her why she was moving.

"The neighbors," she said with vague embarrassment. "Their looks. Their questions. It's simply too much for me."

"And what about Robbie?" I asked gently.

243

Her face bunched up for a second and her lips trembled. "I just can't . . ." She put a hand to her mouth.

"They'll take care of her," she said after a time. "And perhaps someday she'll come back to me."

She held out her hand, and I shook it.

Mildred smiled and said, "Goodbye, Harry."

I walked back out into the sunlight, through that maze of furniture, and down to the street. I stood by the car and stared at the massive stone church on the corner. I thought of the priest and his broomstick. And all that dust.

Then I got in the Pinto and drove away.

JONATHAN VALIN

NATURAL CAUSES   68247-8/$2.95
When ace detective Harry Stoner is hired to find out who
killed a TV soap writer, he uncovers a slick world of high
finance and low morals, the perfect setting for greed,
jealousy, and murder.
"A superior writer...Smart and sophisticated."
The New York Times Book Review

DAY OF WRATH   63917-3/$3.50 US/$4.50 Can
Harry Stoner takes on the simple case of a teenage runaway—and finds himself on a bloody trail leading from the
sleazy barrooms of Cincinnati to the luxurious penthouse
of a well-known socialite.
"An out-and-out shocker." *Chicago Sun-Times*

DEAD LETTER   61366-2/$3.50 US/$4.50 Can
The Cincinnati private eye is pitted against the rivalries
and plots of a hateful family, who soon have him involved
in a gruesome murder case.
"A classic puzzle of motives." *Newsweek*

FINAL NOTICE   57893-X/$3.50 US/$4.50 Can
Private eye Harry Stoner must find a psychotic killer who
mutilates art photos of beautiful women before moving on to
living victims.
"One of the scariest, most pulse-pounding thrillers you'll
ever read...A superior mystery." *Booklist*

LIME PIT   55442-9/$3.50 US/$4.50 Can
Harry Stoner tries to right the wrongs of a heartless city
as he searches for a 16-year-old runaway who has disappeared into Cincinnati's seamy netherworld of prostitution
and porn.
"THE LIME PIT is done right!" *New York Daily News*